OUT OF THIS WORLD

Douglas E. Richards

Paragon Press

Copyright © 2012 by Douglas E. Richards

ParagonPressSF@gmail.com

Author's E-mail address: doug@san.rr.com. Feel free to Friend Douglas on Facebook at Douglas E. Richards Author, or visit his website at www.douglaserichards.com

ISBN: 978-0-9853503-4-5

Library of Congress Control Number: 2012911770

First Edition

Printed in the United States of America

ABOUT THE AUTHOR

Douglas E. Richards is the *New York Times* and *USA Today* bestselling author of the adult science fiction thriller *WIRED*, and its sequel, *AMPED*. He has also written six middle grade/young adult novels widely acclaimed for their appeal to boys, girls, and adults alike. In 2010, in recognition of his work, he was selected to be a "special guest" at San Diego Comic-Con International, along with such icons as Stan Lee, Ray Bradbury, and Rick Riordan. Richards has written numerous feature articles for the award-winning magazine, *National Geographic KIDS*—some having appeared in a dozen languages in as many as sixteen countries—as well as for *American Fencing Magazine*. He currently lives in San Diego, California with his wife, two children, and two dogs.

ALSO BY DOUGLAS E RICHARDS

Adult

WIRED (sci-fi/technothriller)

AMPED (the *WIRED* sequel)

Middle Grade/YA

The Prometheus Project: Trapped (Book 1)

The Prometheus Project: Captured (Book 2)

The Prometheus Project: Stranded (Book 3)

The Devil's Sword

Ethan Pritcher, Body Switcher

OUT OF THIS WORLD

Douglas E. Richards

Paragon Press

CHAPTER ONE

The Amazing Zacharini

Zachary Lane carefully scooped up the deck of cards in front of him on his bedroom floor and held them against his forehead. He shut his eyes and squinted in pretend concentration. "And now," he whispered mystically, "the *Amazing Zacharini* will use the power of his colossal mind to find the card you picked. Using brainwaves alone."

He opened his eyes and stared intently into the hazel eyes of his sister, Jenna, two years younger, seated on the tan carpet across from him. Her face had a smattering of light freckles and she had shoulder length, brownish-blonde hair.

Jenna was unimpressed. She produced an exaggerated, pretend yawn. "Can you wake me up when this is over, Amazing Zucchini?"

"*Zacharini*" he shot back, annoyed. "You know, like Houdini."

Jenna rolled her eyes. "So you're gonna figure out which card I picked by brainwaves alone, huh?" she said skeptically.

"That's right."

"Don't you have to have a *brain* to do that, Zucchini?" she said with a smirk, trying to get under his skin. Not that she had much chance of succeeding. No one was as sure of himself as Zachary. Her brother thought there was nothing that he couldn't do. And what annoyed Jenna the most was that he was probably *right*. Her parents were both scientists with minds sharp as razors, but she was pretty sure that her brother Zachary was even sharper.

"Really, Jen? That's the best you've got?" he said, shaking his head in pity. "Ten minutes from now, after I've pulled off something truly amazing," he added, raising his eyebrows, "I want you to remember that you said *I* was the one without the brain."

"You're not as amazing as you think you are, Zucchini," said Jenna. "You know what magic trick I'd really like to see?" she added.

"Let me guess," said Zachary without hesitation. "You'd like to see me disappear."

Jenna winced before she could catch herself. She hadn't really wanted him to give her an answer—especially the *right* answer. "No. That wasn't what I was going to say at all," she lied, but she was sure she had said it so pathetically that her brother wouldn't be fooled for a second. Still, there was no turning back now. "You couldn't be more . . . um . . . wrong. You'd better check those magic brainwaves of yours."

Zachary shook his head. "If you'd let me get on with the trick," he said impatiently, "we could all find out just how magic my brainwaves turn out to be."

Jenna frowned. As usual, her attempts at insulting him hadn't worked at all, and may have even backfired. She nodded. "Okay, Zucchini, show me your dumb trick."

Zachary removed the deck of cards from his forehead and held them about a foot off the ground, so all of the cards were facing down. His blue eyes sparkled with amusement as he flipped over the top card and dropped it face-up on the carpet between them. It was the Five of Diamonds.

He ran a hand through his short, light-brown hair and massaged his own head for a moment as if trying to stimulate his brain. "No," he said finally, shaking his head. "That's not your card."

He flipped over the next card from the top of the deck, revealing its identity, and placed it beside the Five. It was the Ace of Spades. He studied it carefully. "No," he said once again.

Jenna tried to act bored but was fascinated despite herself. She watched her brother lay six more cards, face up, beside the first two, each time shaking his head and repeating the word, "No".

And then the moment of truth arrived. Zachary turned over the King of Clubs. *The King of Clubs.* This was the card she had chosen and then returned to the deck. This was the card whose identity she had written down on a piece of paper, now shoved in her pocket, so there could be no cheating. Jenna was careful not to change her expression in any way.

Zachary stared into the King's face intently. He squinted. His forehead creased with concentration. "No," he said finally, shaking his head. He placed the King face-up on the floor with the rest of the cards, and immediately shifted his gaze back to the top of the deck still in his hand.

No? Jenna fought to suppress a smile, but the corners of her mouth turned up slightly even so. *He had said no. Hah.* He didn't know the King was her card, which meant he had botched the trick. He wasn't infallible after all. She fought to hide her excitement. She could hardly wait for the Amazing Zucchini to guess the wrong card so she could rub it in.

Zachary continued turning over cards from the top of the deck, one by one, and staring intently at each. Five more times he said "no" before adding each card to the ever-growing number spread out on the carpet.

He went to flip yet another card, but when he touched the top of the deck his hand jerked back explosively, as if he had received an electric jolt. "Ah-ha," he announced triumphantly. "This was the sign I've been waiting for."

He returned his hand to the deck and lifted the top card in preparation to flip it over and reveal its identity. He stared intently at his sister. "I'll bet you a dollar that the next card I flip over is your card."

Jenna's breath caught in her throat. She had no idea what card he now held in his hand, but she knew one thing for sure: it was *not* the King of Clubs. *She had him.*

Or did she?

She paused in thought. She had bet with Zachary two other times within the last year. Both times he offered her ridiculous bets he couldn't possibly win. Not in a million years. She had been absolutely certain about this: right up until the time that he did, in fact, win. Both bets.

She had better be careful.

Her mind drifted back to a cold, dark night seven months earlier. He had called her into his bedroom and put his hand on the light-switch that controlled his only light. "I'll bet you five dollars that I'm fast enough to turn off this switch and make it to the stairs before my room gets dark."

"What? You're out of your mind."

"Nope. Just superhumanly fast. You know, to go along with all of my other superhuman qualities."

Jenna glanced at the stairs, which were a good fifteen feet away. Saying nothing, she moved her hand to where his had been and flicked the light-switch down. She and her brother were instantly plunged into total darkness.

"Impossible," she said simply.

"Then make the bet," he challenged.

"It's *impossible*, Zack. You'd have to use some kind of trick." She tilted her head in thought. "What did you do, rig a remote control to turn off the lights? So you can do it while you're *already* standing on the stairs?"

"*Jen*," he said, pretending to be offended. "That would be *cheating*. I would *never* do that. I'll stand right where you are and flip the switch with my own hand. Really."

Jenna tested the light switch a few more times and then shrugged. "Okay," she said at last. "You're on. Five dollars." She stepped aside. "Go ahead, Zack. Flip the switch and make it to the stairs before it gets dark. I can't *wait* to see this."

Zachary grinned. "Funny that you say that, Jen. Because I'm afraid you're going to have to."

"Have to what?"

"Have to wait. You didn't think I was going to do this right now, did you?"

Jenna's eyebrows came together in confusion.

"I never said I was going to do it *now*. That was never part of the bet. I'll let you know when I'm ready."

The next morning, Zachary was ready. He opened his window shade and his room was immediately flooded with sunlight. He then calmly switched off the room light, which in broad daylight did not, of course, cause the room to get dark, and walked slowly, deliberately, from the light-switch to the stairs. This *impossible* bet had turned out surprisingly easy for him to win.

Four months later he removed three enormous glasses from the cupboard and filled them to the brim with water. He bet her he could finish drinking all three giant glasses before she could finish drinking a tiny paper cup full of water. There was only one catch: she had to let him finish his first glass and begin to drink his second before she could start.

Jenna remembered the light-switch bet and vowed not to be fooled again. It only took a few seconds for her to figure out his plan. He would knock over her cup while he was getting his head start and claim victory when she wasn't able to drink all of the spilled water. *Not this time*, she thought to herself. This time she'd make sure his plan backfired.

"Okay," she said as innocently as she could. "You have a bet."

"Great," said Zachary, reaching for his first glass.

Jenna blocked his hand. "Wait just a second," she said, smiling slyly. "I have a condition. We can't touch each other's glasses. Whoever does loses instantly."

Zachary looked horrified. "What?"

"You heard me. What's the matter, Zack? You weren't planning to spill my cup were you? You weren't planning to cheat?"

Her brother gulped. "No. Of course not."

"Then you shouldn't have any problem with this."

Zachary grimaced, and Jenna could tell he was frantically searching to find a way to escape her trap. But there was no way out. *He* was the one who had proposed the bet, and he couldn't possibly argue that her condition was unreasonable.

"Well?" pressed Jenna.

Her brother considered for a moment longer and then nodded miserably.

"That's more like it," she said happily. She waved her hand toward his large glasses of water and grinned. "Let's get started."

Zachary reached for his first glass and slowly began drinking. And he didn't look happy. Jenna readied herself to snatch her tiny cup and drain it the moment her brother began to drink from his next glass, as they had agreed.

Zachary reached for his second glass. He was just inches from it . . . and then stopped.

And then stopped.

Instead of touching his second glass he picked up the first again, the one he had just emptied, and grinned at his sister. Raising his eyebrows mischievously, he turned the empty glass over and swiftly brought it down over Jenna's paper cup. Then he calmly reached for his second glass and began drinking.

Jenna shook her head in confusion. *How lame.* He had delayed her for a moment, but he still didn't have a chance. She could drain this tiny cup in a single gulp before he even started on his third glass. She reached out to remove her cup from the prison of her brother's overturned glass.

"I wouldn't do that if I were you," warned Zachary, who had suddenly stopped drinking.

"What are you talking about?"

Zachary shook his head. "I can't believe you would forget your own rule. Remember? We can't touch each other's glasses or we lose. You weren't just about to touch my glass, were you?"

Her face contorted into a mask of horror as she realized how completely she had fallen into Zachary's trap, and how foolproof it was. He hadn't broken any rules. His glass hadn't touched her cup nor had he caused a single drop to spill from it—but he had left her with no way to reach her tiny container. Worse still, he had tricked her into setting the trap for *herself*. She had become snared on a rule that *she* had insisted upon.

Jenna screamed in frustration as her brother calmly finished his third glass and held out his hand for payment.

Even now, months later, the memory of these humiliating losses still stung; still caused her face to redden in anger.

But that was then and this was now.

She looked at the cards again and considered the bet her brother was offering. This situation was different from the last two. This wasn't a preplanned con. This was a stupid magic trick he was trying to teach himself.

And he only wanted to bet a dollar, not five or more, which showed that he wasn't too sure of himself.

And there was no way out this time.

The next card he turned over couldn't be hers because he had *already* turned hers over. This was her chance to get even with him for the last two bets. Maybe *more* than even.

"Why just a dollar?" she asked. "Let's make this interesting."

Jenna Lane leaned forward and stared intently at her older brother. "I'll bet you a *hundred* dollars!" she challenged firmly.

CHAPTER TWO

A Winning Bet

Zachary coughed. "A . . . a hundred bucks. Have you gone crazy?"

"What's wrong, Amazing Zucchini? Don't tell me you're losing your touch."

Her brother frowned. "You're insane, skunk-breath. Besides, you don't have a hundred dollars."

Jenna considered. He was right. He had been saving his allowance money for a long time, but she hadn't. "Then you put up a hundred and I'll put up whatever you want. How about my bike?"

Zachary shook his head. "What would I do with your bike? I'll tell you what: if I lose I'll give you the hundred. But if *you* lose, you have to do my chores for three months."

"Which ones?"

"All of them. Whenever it's my turn to do the dishes, take out the garbage, rake leaves—whatever—you have to do it for me."

Jenna glanced at the cards Zachary had already turned over for reassurance and was comforted to see the King of Clubs still among them. "You're on," she said, barely able to contain her excitement. She trained her eyes on the deck in his hand and the card he was holding by its edge. "Flip it over and let's see."

Zachary smiled triumphantly. "You know something, Jenna," he said. "After you've done the last chore for me three months from now, as a favor to you, I'm going to teach you how to stop making losing bets."

"Yeah, yeah, yeah. The first thing I'm going to do with the hundred dollars I *win* is buy you a muzzle. Why don't you just turn over the stupid card already and quit stalling."

A wide grin came over Zachary's face. "Okay, Jen. Whatever you want," he said smugly. "You're going to *love* this." He paused. "I will now flip over your card," he announced theatrically, using the voice of the Amazing Zacharini once again.

He pulled the top card from the deck and moved it, its face still down, closer to Jenna. Then he began the motion as though he would flip it over—and then stopped.

And then stopped.

He brought the card back to the top of the deck and replaced it there. He lowered the deck and set it down on the carpet.

And then, as Jenna's jaw dropped to the floor, Zachary reached forward, grabbed the King of Clubs where it had rested on the carpet between them now for several minutes, and flipped it back over the *other way*, so the card's back was all that could be seen.

She gasped in surprise and horror. *He had done it again.*

He had said that her card would be the next card he turned over. He had never said that it would necessarily be the one from the top of the deck he had been holding, just because all the others had been. And he had never said it couldn't be one he had *already* turned over.

"I really, really hate you," said Jenna through clenched teeth. "Not only that," she continued, "but did I mention that I hate you?"

"I'm sorry you feel that way, Jen. I've always thought you were . . . well . . . just the best," he gushed sarcastically. "Especially now that you're going to be helping me so much. I couldn't ask for a better sister."

At that exact instant their mother walked into the room, just in time to hear Zachary's last sentence. "Zack, what a nice thing to say to Jenna. It's great to see you two getting along so well," she said happily.

Jenna fumed silently.

"We're having dinner in five minutes," announced Mrs. Lane, who had shorter hair and fewer freckles than Jenna, but similar coloring and features.

"Hey Mom," said Zachary, "isn't it my turn to do the dishes tonight?"

Mrs. Lane looked at her son as if he had come from another planet. "As a matter of fact, it is," she answered. "But I never thought I would live to see the day when *you* would be reminding *me* of that."

Zachary smirked and glanced at his sister whose face was so red with fury that he thought she would explode. He could swear steam was coming from her ears. "Well, we all have to do our part, don't we," he said.

"Unbelievable," said his stunned mother as she left his room and headed for the stairs, shaking her head.

Jenna and Zachary waited until their mom was out of hearing distance to pick up where they had left off.

"*You are such an enormous jerk!*" spat Jenna. "I should have known. How could I have fallen for another one of your scams? I must be the biggest idiot in the world!" she continued in frustration.

And she *was*. Her brother was always so clever while she was so . . . not clever. Somehow none of her parents' talents had been passed to her. That's why she rarely put effort into anything. Why bother? She couldn't measure up to the rest of her family no matter what she did. She just had to face facts—Zachary had gotten a double dose of the Lane smart genes and she had gotten none.

"Don't be so hard on yourself, Jen," said Zachary smoothly. "You're not the *biggest* idiot in the world. I mean, there must be *one* person who's a bigger idiot than you." He held out his hands, palms up. "I mean, I can't think of anyone at the moment. But there must be *someone* . . ."

His sister glared at him with a savage intensity.

"Hey," said Zachary innocently. "You shouldn't be angry. I'm only hurting myself. You know how Mom and Dad are always saying that doing chores builds character." He grinned. "Well, you'll be building *a lot of* character." He lowered his eyes and looked sad, "While I'll be ruining my life playing video games and watching movies."

"You think you're so cool," growled Jenna. "But I notice you didn't say you'd be playing with your *friends*, did you? Because you barely have any."

For just an instant Jenna thought she had landed a blow, that she had detected a flash of uncertainty, or even anguish, on Zack's face, but she couldn't be sure. And since his face was now back to its natural state of absolute confidence, she could well have imagined it.

"There is one other thing," said Zachary, clearly deciding to ignore what Jenna had just said. "Well, *two* other things. What do you want first, the good news or the bad?"

"Neither," she said. "I'm leaving. You may have won the bet, but that doesn't mean I have to listen to your garbage for even a second longer."

"Yeah, well this has to do with the bet," said Zachary. "So I'll make it quick, and then you can go. I'll start with the good news. I tried to pull this same scam on Dad earlier today. But he won the bet. He figured out what I was going to do and messed me up."

It figured, thought Jenna. If anyone could beat Zachary at his own game, it would be their dad. "How is that good news?"

Zachary shrugged. "I figured you'd like hearing that I got beaten."

Jenna had to admit he had a point. "So how did he win?" she asked. She could see someone figuring out what her brother was going to do, but she couldn't figure how anyone could take the bet and actually win.

"Good question. Until I tried it on Dad I couldn't think of a way either. But Dad sure did. The second he accepted the bet he grabbed all the cards already face-up on the floor and turned them all over. Then he mixed them up, looked at me, and said, 'Okay, Son, now turn over my card.'"

Jenna grinned. "Wow. Dad really turned the tables on you." She only wished she could have seen the look on her brother's face when it had happened. "So what did you lose?" she asked.

Now it was Zachary's turn to smile. "Funny you should ask that. That's the *bad news* part. At least for you. Dad didn't want to bet money. So we ended up betting . . . well . . . chores. If I won, I wouldn't be given any for the next three months. If Dad won, I would have to take on twice as many." He paused. "As you know . . . I lost."

Zachary looked at his sister in mock sympathy as he stood up from the floor. "I'm afraid it's going to be a long three months for you, Sis."

Jenna gasped in horror as the full, nightmarish implications of what her brother just said hit her like a freight train. *Triple chores.*

Zachary darted through the open doorway as his sister began screaming—just managing to dodge the shoe she had thrown at him with surprising velocity.

CHAPTER THREE

Vanished

Jenna's father and brother were already seated at the kitchen table when she made it downstairs several minutes later. Upon seeing her arrive, her mother set a large white casserole dish on the table filled with what looked like Chicken Tetrazzini, although it was difficult to be sure. An unusual and unappealing scent rose from the dish and attacked Jenna's nostrils. Mrs. Lane may have been a talented chemist, but for some reason her talents didn't extend into the kitchen. Jenna's father was a much better cook but he only cooked every other meal.

Mr. Lane was a short man with dark brown hair and a round, friendly face, who always seemed to have a twinkle in his hazel eyes. He eyed the mystery meal cautiously, plopped a pungent mound of it onto his plate, and made a weak attempt to pretend to be enthusiastic about eating it.

"Jenna, Sweetheart," he said, looking concerned as she seated herself at the table. "I could have sworn I heard screaming coming from upstairs. Is everything okay?"

Jenna sighed. "Just fine, Dad. Besides, I didn't hear any screaming."

"That's what your brother said."

Zachary looked at his sister innocently and shrugged his shoulders as if to say, *isn't it strange that Dad thought he heard something.*

"The kids were upstairs playing," reported Mrs. Lane to their father. She turned to face her children. "I'm glad to see it. It's a nice change from all that sparring you two always seem to be doing."

"Mom, *really*," said Zachary, pretending to be offended. "You make what we do sound like a *bad* thing. Think of it more as . . . well, as verbal dueling. It's good for us. You know, like being on the debate team. It's helped make me the totally awesome human being that I am today."

Mr. Lane shook his head as he took a tentative forkful of what he hoped was chicken. "You know, not even a cow pasture is as full of manure as you are."

"Cow pasture?" said Zachary with a wry smile. "Manure? Really? Was that the cool expression a hundred years ago, Dad?"

"No. I just made it up. How would you have said it?"

Zachary thought about it for just a moment. "How about, not even a porta-potty is as full of cra . . ."

"Okay, okay," interrupted Mr. Lane. "Regardless of the expression you use, my point is that you're full of it. Fighting with Jenna is like being on the debate team? Now I've heard everything."

"I'm telling you, our sparring is a good thing," continued Zachary, undeterred. "It's giving us a chance to hone our linguistic skills—very educational." He smiled. "There, did you see. I just used the words hone and linguistic. It's obviously working."

His father didn't respond. He simply rolled his eyes and shook his head in disbelief.

"Or think of it this way," continued Zachary. "You've seen animal documentaries. Young animals play-fight with each other to learn important hunting skills they'll need to survive when they're adults. That's all Jen and I are doing. We're just testing out our verbal combat skills to use in the human jungle we'll find ourselves in when we're older. Isn't it obvious that Jen and I love each other to death?" he finished with exaggerated sweetness, glancing over at his sister and fluttering his eyelashes.

"*PaaLeeese*, Zack," she pleaded. "I'm eating. If your goal is to *hone* your verbal skills to the point where you can use them to make people puke—trust me, you're already there."

Zachary smiled and looked at his dad. "See. I rest my case. See how I've inspired my lame sister to come up with a halfway decent insult?" He raised his hands in front of him and turned his head in a show of modesty.

"But no need to thank me for helping to mold your daughter. Really."

Mrs. Lane smiled. "Well, we know one thing for sure. If you can't get a real job, you'll always be able to get one as a conman."

"Or at least as a carnival pitchman," his father chimed in.

"Or maybe a used car salesman," added Jenna.

"You'd make a fine lab rat," continued Mrs. Lane.

"Now I think you've gone too far," said Mr. Lane. "I don't think he's furry enough to make a good lab rat."

"Hey," complained Zachary. "I'm being ganged up on. I don't have to sit here and take this."

Zachary's father pursed his lips. "Well, actually . . . you do. Just think of it as Mom and I working to *hone* you. You know, just like in the animal kingdom. Working to teach you survival skills."

"Yeah, but with you and Mom, I can't *hone* back or I get grounded."

"True enough," agreed Mr. Lane whimsically. "That does tend to give us the upper hand."

Jenna laughed. The conversation had put her in a much better mood. Her parents had a way of doing that.

"Well that was, ah . . . delicious," said Mr. Lane, pushing his plate forward. "Thank you so much, Honey."

Mrs. Lane eyed her husband dubiously and then turned to her children. "Did you hate it too?"

Zachary and Jenna looked at each other helplessly. "No Mom," replied Jenna finally. "It was . . . it was great."

Mrs. Lane smiled. "Yeah, just as I thought. I hated it too. Just because I cooked it doesn't mean that I don't have any taste buds. This won't get added to the list of regular meals."

The Lane family let out a collective sigh of relief.

"Mom, I know that you're an experimental chemist," said Zachary wryly, putting on a pained expression. "But do you have to experiment with *dinner?*"

Everyone laughed, including Zachary's mother. Still smiling, she stood up and moved to where her husband was sitting. The white casserole dish was in front of him, filled with her horrible meal, and she decided it was time to remove it from the table.

The kitchen began shimmering wildly.

Shimmering?

Jenna's eyes widened in dismay.

Rooms should definitely *not* shimmer. The kitchen seemed to undulate and it was distorted the way things were when you looked at them underwater while you were swimming. Or how the air sometimes looked around a blazing fire: all wavy and quivery. Was she the only one who was experiencing it?

She looked over at her parents to find out. *And they disappeared.*

Jenna heard a *Zzzt, Zzzt, Zzzt* sound—like the sound an electric bug-zapper made when it was zapping a bug—and watched in horror as her parents sank into the floor and were gone.

Zzzt, Zzzt, Zzzt.

Her parents had somehow been swallowed by the floor.

They had disappeared right in front of her eyes, as if a trap door had suddenly opened beneath them and plunged them into a bottomless pit.

Jenna gasped as the kitchen lights began to flicker and the room continued its unearthly shimmering.

CHAPTER FOUR

The Portal

Jenna bolted out of her chair in horror. "Mom! Dad!" she yelled frantically. She had been seated closest to her father and rushed forward to where her parents had disappeared. But just before she reached her destination she realized that whatever had swallowed her parents was still there. She froze in place and looked down.

And not an instant too soon. She was teetering at the edge of a huge, shimmering hole. The front halves of her shoes had already disappeared into this vast nothingness. And she was tipping forward. She gasped, swinging her arms in big circles, fighting to regain her balance. But she couldn't do it. She continued to fall forward into the hole.

In that brief instant she knew she was done for.

From behind her, Zachary's arms shot out and wrapped around her waist as she fell. Using all of his strength he stopped her momentum and launched the two of them backwards. He landed with a thud on the hardwood floor, sprawled out on his back, and his sister crashed down on top of him, the back of her head whip-lashing into his jaw.

It had all happened in the blink of an eye and Jenna was temporarily stunned. While her heart continued to race furiously the rest of her was paralyzed. She slowly came to her senses and realized that Zachary had long since removed his arms from around her waist and she was still on top of him. She quickly rolled off. Her brother was gingerly massaging his sore jaw.

"Sorry," she said breathlessly. "Are you okay?"

He nodded, sitting up and carefully brushing over her legs and feet with both hands to satisfy himself that she was still in one piece. "Whew," he said. "I thought you were a goner for a second."

Jenna sat up. "So did I." A tear escaped from the corner of her eye and trickled slowly down her face as the enormity of everything that was happening caught up to her. "Zack—" She was at a loss for words. "Thanks."

"Well I couldn't have you disappearing on me," he said awkwardly.

Jenna frowned deeply as her thoughts turned again to her parents. *They were gone.* Just like that.

"Zack, what— " she croaked, barely managing to hold herself together. "What happened to Mom and Dad?"

The color had drained from Zachary's face and he looked ill. "I don't know," he replied gravely, and Jenna could see that his eyes were moist like her own.

Jenna had seen her brother when he had injured himself, and had seen him face any number of difficult situations, and he always stayed cool and focused. She couldn't remember the last time he had shown this depth of emotion. Having just watched his parents disappear into thin air and almost losing his sister to this same fate had shaken him badly.

But as Jenna watched, her brother pulled himself together. He gritted his teeth and his expression hardened. "I don't know what's going on. But whatever it is—we're going to find out."

Zachary jumped to his feet and motioned for Jenna to join him. They stood at the edge of the hole that had swallowed their parents and looked down. It was a perfect circle, about ten feet in diameter, and it shimmered wildly as if it were a field of energy. When they looked directly at the field their eyes blurred and they couldn't keep their focus. But if they tried to look *through* it, rather than *at* it, it became as clear as glass.

And somehow, this energy window in their kitchen floor didn't show their basement below, but rather rolling hills and countryside, as clear as a bell for many miles. There was a road winding through the green hills and a bright red farmhouse in the distance. And even though they were looking down through the portal they viewed the scene sideways, as if from a car window.

Their mouths hung open in fascination and disbelief. *How could this be?*

Jenna spotted a small, bright purple bird flying towards her. Bright purple? As it got closer she saw that in addition to its unusual color the bird's body was so plump it formed almost a perfect sphere. It was the most ridiculous looking bird she had ever seen: a feather-covered, stubby-winged, purple softball flying through the air. She followed it in fascination as it got closer and closer and—

"Ahhh" she yelled, throwing her head to the side as the bird came hurtling through the shimmering portal, passing right through the exact spot her head had been only a moment before. The bird barely managed to stop before hitting the ceiling and then, finally, landed with a thud on the kitchen table on legs as short and stubby as its wings.

The bird turned toward the stunned kids and began looking them up and down.

"Now what?" asked Jenna.

"I don't know," answered her brother. "But at this point, nothing in the world could possibly surprise me."

"Hello, kids," said the bird matter-of-factly.

They both gasped in dismay. The bird's beak had moved but *their mother's* voice had come out.

"I have a message for you."

CHAPTER FIVE

The Mimic Bird

Okay, thought Zachary, nothing in the world could possibly surprise me—*except Mom turning into a bird.* He suddenly felt dizzy and put a hand on the kitchen table to steady himself. Jenna had sunk to the floor, her mouth still hanging open.

"Don't worry," continued the bird in their mother's voice. "I haven't turned into a bird. And I wasn't eaten by one, either."

Both kids let out a sigh of relief. But how had the bird known what they were thinking? It must be psychic.

"And I can't read minds, either," said the bird, reading their minds. "Your Dad and I just took a guess at the first few things that would pop into your minds when this bird started talking."

Suddenly, they both realized that what the bird was saying was not nearly as important as the reason the bird was there. That meant everything.

It meant that their parents were alive.

They both began speaking at once. "Who are you? How can you talk? Why do you sound just like Mom? Are Mom and Dad okay?"

"I'm sure you have a thousand questions to ask," continued their small purple visitor. "Unfortunately, the bird that is talking to you can't answer them. It's only a bird, after all, and not very intelligent. It's called a Mimic Bird—for obvious reasons. Think of it as a living tape-recorder. It can only repeat the exact words your father and I had it memorize, using our voices. That's what it's doing right now. We trained it—using the pictures of you Dad has in his wallet—to replay this message once it found you. Unfortunately, its memory capacity isn't great so we had better get right to it."

Jenna and Zachary looked at each other and both raised their eyebrows. Of course. Why hadn't they guessed? This was a Mimic Bird. At this point it wasn't any crazier than anything else that had just happened.

The bird continued. "We're so sorry it's taken us so long to find a way to get a message to you, but we've done the best we could."

Zachary's eyes widened. *So long?* They had disappeared just four or five minutes earlier.

"We're guessing we've been gone about ten days—"

"*Ten days!*" shouted Jenna in shock.

"—But we're not exactly sure," continued the bird. "And we don't know how long it's taken the bird to find you. We've been worried sick. But Catherine, we just know you've been doing a fantastic job taking care of Zachary and Jenna while we've been gone. We'll never be able to thank you enough—or tell you how sorry we are that this happened."

The siblings glanced at each other in confusion. Catherine? *Aunt* Catherine? They hadn't seen her in a few weeks.

"We miss you so much," continued the bird. "And we can only imagine how worried you must have been all this time not knowing what happened to us. And the worst of it is, *we're* still not sure exactly what happened to us." The bird paused, twisting its head around and using its beak to attend to some feathers on its left wing.

When the bird spoke next, it was using their father's voice. "All we know is that a strange hole somehow appeared in our kitchen and we fell in. Well, we didn't really fall. I guess we passed through it—like a door or a portal. One moment we were in our kitchen and the next . . . and the next we weren't even on Earth anymore. We can't say what world we landed on, but it definitely wasn't Earth."

The bird paused. "Since then we've gone through many more of these portals, trying to find our way back to you. As far as we can tell, each one leads to a different place, on a different world. Some of the places look like they could be on Earth, but they're all inhabited by the strangest people and creatures you can imagine. This talking bird in front of you is only one example. But no matter how much we try to question the intelligent beings we run into, no one or no-thing can explain to us what's going on. We don't know if we're somehow traveling between different planets, or if we're traveling to other dimensions from our own. Or it could be something else. Something we can't even begin to imagine."

The bird paused for air. "Each world is much different from the others," it continued. "And each is unbelievably strange. Most of the worlds are treacherous; containing hostile environments or even more hostile natives. But even the worlds that appear harmless have not been—by any means. Surviving each day has been a constant challenge. It's taken all of our physical strength and wits to stay alive."

The living tape recorder switched again to their mother's voice. "Unfortunately, after all this time, we haven't made much progress. We're not sure we're any closer to understanding what's happening or to making it back than when we started." The bird paused. "But please don't worry about us. We *will* discover a way out of this and come back to you. In the meanwhile, you are both fantastic kids, and we're counting on you to stay strong and look out for each other. You know how very much we love you," said the bird, exactly copying their mother's voice when she had spoken these words, soft and choked-up with emotion.

The bird continued in their father's voice. "Unfortunately, we think the bird is running out of memory, so we can't say much more. Before we go, though, we have one more important message for all of you. Whatever you do, *don't come in after us!* We can't stress this enough. Do *not* come in after us—under *any* circumstances. It's far, far, too treacherous." The bird paused. "And Catherine, we just want you to know that— "

The bird stopped in mid sentence.

Zachary looked at it in annoyance. "Go on," he urged.

"Go on," said the bird, sounding exactly like Zachary. It was eerie.

"I think it ran out of memory," said Jenna. "Like Mom and Dad guessed."

"I think it ran out of memory. Like Mom and Dad guessed," repeated the bird, this time using Jenna's voice.

"Interesting," said Zachary. "It must have erased Mom and Dad's message and is memorizing what we say."

"Interesting," said the bird. "It must have erased Mom and Dad's message and is memorizing what we say."

Zachary looked at his sister and rolled his eyes. *Let's get rid of this thing*, he mouthed silently so the bird wouldn't repeat him. *It's really starting to get on my nerves.*

His sister nodded in agreement as Zachary extended his hand toward the bird and it dutifully jumped onto his arm.

That was easy, he thought. He walked to the edge of the portal and shook it off gently. The bird took the hint and in seconds it had disappeared through the ever-shimmering portal.

Jenna and Zachary gazed through the portal and watched the bird's awkward flight for several seconds.

With the bird gone they retreated from the portal, both deep in thought. Jenna broke the silence. "Zack, how could Mom and Dad have been gone for ten days?"

Zachary shook his head. "I don't know," he mumbled. "It's impossible. But I guess it's no more impossible than this hole appearing in our kitchen. Or getting a visit from a living tape-recorder."

"Why did they think Aunt Catherine was with us?"

"Because if they really had been gone as long as they thought, she *would've* been. They knew that Aunt Catherine would've been the first person we called. And if they weren't back in a few days, she'd have moved in with us."

Jenna nodded. That made sense. "Well, now that you mention it, we *should* call her. Right away. We have to let her know what happened. And then we should call the police."

Zachary frowned. He had come to a conclusion that he didn't like, but one that was inescapable. He took a deep breath, let it out slowly, and faced his sister. "No, Jen. You and I have to go in after them," he said as bravely as he could. "It's the only way."

"What!"

"We have to Jen."

"But you heard Mom and Dad. That's the one thing they told us *not* to do," she reminded him. "No matter what."

"I know that. They also told us they'd make it back and not to worry. But that's because they don't want us to panic. They're in big, big trouble."

"I *know*. But if it's so dangerous, how can we help? We're just kids. We need to call the police. Maybe even the army." Her face brightened. "That's it. The army. They can bring Mom and Dad back if anyone can."

"That's true," said Zachary. "But there's no time. Think about it. The bird came back through the portal about five minutes after they disappeared. Time for us is running at a different speed than time for them. Ten days for Mom and Dad is only four or five minutes for us. That means that while we've been listening to that bird and talking, ten or twenty more days have already gone by for them." Zachary lowered his eyes. "And they're not back," he continued somberly. "How much longer do you think they can last? And even if they find a safe world, at the rate time is running for them, if they haven't made it back by tomorrow, they'll have died from old age." He shook his head. "By the time Aunt Catherine or anyone else gets here it could be too late. We have to act *now*."

Jenna felt sick to her stomach as his point hit home. He was right. It might be too late for their parents already.

She and her brother had experienced the same events, and both had the same facts, but he had been able to see so much more.

She pointed toward the portal. "But if Mom and Dad can barely survive these worlds and can't figure out how to get back—how can we?"

"I'm not sure. Maybe the natives that gave Mom and Dad such a hard time will give us a break because we're kids. Maybe this will give us a chance to find Mom and Dad and figure out a way to return. I don't know. I only know that we have to *try*," he finished, determined.

Jenna lowered her eyes. "Then you should go alone. I'll just slow you down."

"What?"

"Look, Zachary, let's face it, I'm pretty much of an idiot. You'll stand a better chance alone."

"Come on Jenna, we don't have time to kid around."

A tear escaped from the corner of Jenna's eyes and rolled slowly down her cheek. Zachary rarely noticed the emotions or body language of those around him, but it was impossible to miss what this meant. Jenna was *serious*. "Jen, you really think you're *stupid*? How could you be so stupid as to think you're stupid?" he added in exasperation.

"Yeah. I wonder," said Jenna as another tear escaped her eye. "It's not like you haven't been reminding me a hundred times a day since I was born. You just said an hour ago that you couldn't think of anyone on the planet more stupid than me."

Zachary shook his head as if to clear it. It was true he teased her a lot, but he never thought she took him seriously. Didn't all brothers tease their sisters? "Jenna, don't be crazy," he said. "I think you're very bright. I mean your grades are only okay, not great, but that's because you're lazy. If you can't figure something out in a few seconds you just stop trying. But I live with you, and I see how you solve problems. You get puns and jokes faster than anyone in my class. And you even beat me at Boggle sometimes." Zachary grimaced. He was so competitive that even the memory of these losses was painful. "And no-one else ever has. Not even Mom or Dad."

"Zachary, this is too important for you to lie to me. Yeah, I get lucky at Boggle sometimes, but you know you're a ton brighter than I am. You'll do much better alone."

Zachary stared into her eyes. How had he not seen how little she thought of her own abilities? His insults must have been even sharper than he had thought. And the poor kid was in his shadow at school. And if he did say so himself, he was an incredibly tough act to follow. It would be hard on *anyone*, no matter *how* impressive, to be compared to him every day, he thought.

But he had made this even harder for her by telling her she was an idiot so often. A sick feeling gripped his stomach. How badly had he messed her up? Was he *totally* responsible for her lack of confidence?

Maybe he was. His parents had told him recently they worried he was arrogant—which meant that he had a lot of confidence, but in a bad way. They worried he was too full of himself to even notice the struggles of others. This sure seemed to be true in Jenna's case. And it had taken a disaster—the disappearance of their parents—for him to see it.

His parents had also used the word "smug," and said that this quality could cause people not to like him, even though he was clever and the star pitcher on the baseball team. He had thought they were crazy, but maybe there was some truth to what they had said. Jenna had been right after he had won the card trick bet. He didn't have many friends. And he never seemed to keep the ones he had for very long. Which was surprising, since you'd think *everyone* would want to be friends with someone as impressive as he was.

He wanted to think about this longer, but there was no time. "Okay," he said to his sister. "I get why you'd have trouble believing what I say. But what about Mom and Dad? They're always telling you how talented you are. All your life."

Jenna frowned. "Yeah, but they don't really mean it. Saying stuff like that is just their way of trying to be good parents."

"Come on, Jen. That laser you built with Dad won the science fair competition at school. What about that?"

"Big deal. With Dad's help, of course I'm gonna win." She shook her head. "Look, Zack, even if I'm not a *total* idiot—and I can't believe I'm about to admit this—I'm not even close to being in *your* league. Come on Zack, you know I'm not."

Zachary paused, deep in thought, for what seemed like an eternity. "All right," he said, and a change came over him, as though he had finally decided to share the ultimate secret. "You're right. You're not in my league. But that's not because I'm better than you. It's because you're younger. And because— "

He paused, as if searching for the right words.

"Because what?" said Jenna. "Because I'm a moron?"

"No. Because . . . well, because my natural abilities have been getting a little help the last few years. From one of Mom and Dad's inventions."

"What are you talking about?"

"Look, I don't have time for long explanations. You know Mom and Dad do top secret work. Well, I found out about one of their projects a few years ago. They discovered how to generate some kind of new electro-magnetic waves—ones you can't feel—just like radio and TV waves that are always hitting us but we don't know it. But when these waves hit you, they improve you. I convinced Mom and Dad to let me be one of the test subjects. I've been carrying around a tiny generator one day a week for two years now. That's why I do better than you in school and *that's* why you're not in my league."

Jenna snorted. "I may be gullible, Zachary, but even I'm not *that* gullible. That's the stupidest thing I've ever heard."

"Look, I don't care what you believe. I don't have time to argue. *I'm* going after them. Yes, if we run into trouble, I'll probably be the one who figures a way out. But maybe not *every* time. Our chances are better if you're with me. Really."

Jenna took a deep breath and closed her eyes. Finally, she nodded. "Okay," she said. "Let's do this."

"Great," said Zachary. "Wait here."

Before she could respond he bolted off at full speed up the stairs, taking them two at a time. In seconds he returned. He handed her a small sphere, the size and weight of a golf ball.

Jenna examined it. The outer surface was hard plastic and was transparent. Inside there were a number of what looked like miniature computer chips; tiny black squares with rows of pointy, silver, centipede legs sticking down from their edges. Attached to the silver legs of the computer chips was a complex spaghetti of delicate wires of every color.

"Put it in your pocket."

"What is it?"

"Haven't you been paying attention? It's the wave-field generator Mom and Dad invented. If you carry it for a day the effect lasts the whole week, so I don't need it."

Jenna rolled her eyes.

"Believe what you want," he said. "I don't care. But put it in your pocket anyway. As a favor to me." He pointed toward the portal. "We're headed into dangerous territory and we both have to be at our best to have any hope of finding Mom and Dad and getting back."

Jenna was almost starting to believe him. He sure was taking this secret generator nonsense pretty seriously. And he wouldn't waste time scamming her now. Every second counted. "What does it do?" she asked.

"It broadcasts what Mom and Dad call Omega waves. Mom says these waves interact in some way with the electrical fields generated by our brains. Mom and Dad worked a long time to get the frequency just right. I don't know how, but when the waves hit your brain you can think more clearly, you get more relaxed, and for some reason you can produce adrenaline faster. You know, that's the stuff your body produces that can make you super-strong in emergencies. So it makes you stronger."

"And you have no idea how it works?"

"No. Mom and Dad do, but it's too complicated for me. Something about the field being able to neutralize stray electrical impulses that can confuse your thoughts. Basically, it clears the electrical gunk away from the circuitry in your brain."

"Is that the scientific term for it? Gunk?" asked Jenna sarcastically.

"Give me a break, will you! Whatever it does, it lets your brain operate faster, and helps you think more clearly. All I know is that it works."

Frowning, Jenna shoved the ball deep into her front pants pocket and tried hard not to consider the implications of what her brother was saying. How incredible. It sure would explain why Zachary seemed almost superhuman sometimes. Why hadn't her parents told her about this generator? She decided to not waste any energy pondering this development. Far too many things were happening at the same time and she had reached her limit.

She took her brother's hand. "I'm ready," she said thinly as if she were going to her own funeral, which could well turn out to be the truth. "Let's go."

They walked to the edge of the portal holding hands. "Let's jump on three," said Zachary.

They squeezed their eyes shut and tried to control the butterflies in their stomachs, but without any success. "One. Two. Three," said Zachary slowly as they jumped into the center of the portal, each holding their breath as though they were jumping into a pool.

There was no sensation of falling, just of firm ground under their feet. They opened their eyes.

They were through. They had made it. They were on the world they had seen through the portal, standing on the winding, two-lane road.

They were alive—and safe.

Just as they let out the breath they had been holding, relieved, they heard the screech of brakes behind them. They whirled to see a car that had been hurtling around a bend in the road only twenty feet away bearing down upon them.

And there was no way in the world that it could possibly stop before it hit them.

CHAPTER SIX

The Transparent Men

Jenna closed her eyes and braced herself for the impact of the car.

Zachary reacted instantly, diving into his sister and pushing them both out of the car's way as it screeched by them, missing them by mere inches. The dive sent them tumbling headlong down a large, grassy hillside that bordered the road, arms and legs flailing. They landed in a heap at the bottom.

"Owwww," moaned Zachary, moving his sister's foot from its resting place on his neck. They rolled apart and tried to catch their breath while they took inventory of the minor cuts and bruises they had collected on the way down. They were both still slightly dizzy.

"Are you okay?" asked Jenna.

"Yeah, I guess so. Are you?"

Jenna nodded. She was shaken but she would be fine. Thanks to her brother. Where did he get reflexes that fast? And he had been so decisive. Just like in their kitchen when she had almost fallen into the portal. And then she remembered the silly generator he had insisted she carry with her. Maybe there was something to his story, after all. She wondered how long it would take before the Omega waves would start helping her.

"We're not exactly off to a great start," observed Zachary.

"It could have been worse," said Jenna. "A lot worse. And it almost was. Thanks for throwing me off the road."

"No problem," he said. "Although tackling you like that isn't something you usually thank me for," he added with a grin. His expression became serious once again. "We're just lucky that our mission to find Mom and Dad didn't end before it began. We need to really stay alert from now on."

Jenna nodded in agreement as they pulled themselves into a sitting position and looked toward the road on which they had arrived. The car that had almost hit them, a boxy red two-door, had finally come to a full stop about thirty yards beyond where they had briefly been standing. If Zachary hadn't thrown them out of the way they would have ended up as two giant bug-smears on its windshield.

A very tall driver and slightly shorter passenger exited the car and walked to the edge of the road to look down the hill.

Jenna saw them first and gasped. *It couldn't be.*

They appeared to be ordinary men, except for one extraordinary feature.

They were transparent.

YUCK! Jenna almost gagged. Thankfully, both the driver and his passenger were wearing normal pants, but their shirts were transparent and underneath them, so were they. And not just their skin. Their muscles were transparent also. You could see *everything*. All their inner . . . workings.

Even transparent jellyfish gave Jenna the willies, but jellyfish were nothing compared to the sight of these two. This was too much. You could see their skulls and all of their internal organs. Their hearts beating rhythmically. Thump-thump. Thump-thump. Thump-thump. Their lungs filling up with air. Even tiny rivers of blood coursing through their veins and arteries. They were grisly, living illustrations in a medical textbook.

Jenna jabbed her brother in the ribs. "Look up there," she whispered through clenched teeth. "Do you see those guys?"

Zachary did and his mouth dropped open. "Uh-huh," he mumbled. He and his sister instinctively crouched lower to the ground, trying to melt into the hillside so they wouldn't be seen. "I wish I hadn't eaten Mom's disgusting dinner," he whispered, fighting to keep a meal in his stomach that suddenly wanted to come back out. Finally, he was forced to look away from the men to let his stomach settle.

"Uh-oh," whispered Jenna. "We're in trouble."

Zachary glanced up to see the two men walking down the hill, obviously in search of the two kids they had almost hit. Jenna and Zachary held their breath and froze in place. Both men were not only transparent but were also enormous—even the shorter one was over six feet tall.

"Ah," said the taller of the two transparent men, who had been driving. "There you are." He approached quickly from only ten yards away, looking even more repulsive from this short distance. His heart looked like a red fist covered by tiny veins, clenching and unclenching, clenching and unclenching, again and again, pumping blood through the transparent tubes that were his arteries.

"*You speak English?*" said Zachary, astonished.

"Well of course I don't," snapped the man. He handed Zachary a solid purple crystal, about the size of an acorn, that gave off a faint glow. "Place this in your pocket," he instructed as the second transparent man now joined them. "This is a language transformer. It will instantly and automatically transform all possible languages into all other possible languages. Even writing."

"You mean a translator?" said Jenna.

"Were you not listening?" barked the man. "A transformer. If this were a translator you would hear strange sounding words coming from my mouth that this device would then translate into English. Is that what's happening?"

"Ah, no," said Zachary. "It sounds like you're speaking English in the first place."

"Exactly. And I hear you as though you're speaking my language. That is how it works. Not a language translator—a language transformer."

"And it works for writing also?" said Zachary in disbelief.

"Do I need to tell you everything twice?" complained the man. "Yes. Written words, no matter what the language, will look like English to you. And your written words will transform into the language of whoever is reading them."

"How in the world is *that* possible?" asked Zachary skeptically. "It seems more like magic than science."

The taller of the two transparent men shrugged. "Same thing," he said simply.

"*Same thing?*" said Jenna. "Science and magic are the *same thing?*"

The taller transparent man just glared at her but didn't reply. The shorter man—who still soared above them imposingly—stepped forward with a friendly expression. "I can explain," he said. "But first, let me introduce myself. I'm Wyland, and my companion is named Hirth. You are on our world, called Orum."

The kids introduced themselves as well, continuing to look away from the two men periodically. Their transparent bodies were so disgusting, and made the siblings so uneasy, they could only handle looking at them for a few minutes at a time.

"Because we get the occasional visitor from your world," continued Wyland, "we have recently become familiar with what you mean by 'science.' Magic is simply the process of controlling scientific principles with one's mind."

"You're wasting your time!" snapped Hirth. "These humans are feeble-minded and unimaginative. Which is why they can't even use the simplest magic. Why even try to explain?"

Wyland glared at his companion. "I have my reasons," he growled.

This Hirth was really getting under Zachary's skin, but he forced himself not to react to his insult. Zachary didn't believe in magic, of course. But he also didn't believe in portals that could transport you to other worlds, or talking purple birds, so he forced himself to be open minded. "So what science do you activate with your minds to make the language transformer work?" he asked.

Wyland shrugged. "We don't know. You see, although we now realize that magic and science are two sides of the same coin, we have always been able to control magic fairly effortlessly. Without having to really think about it. So just because we can use it doesn't mean we understand what scientific principles we're tapping into."

Zachary looked totally confused.

"I think I get it," said Jenna to her brother. "At least a little. Take gravity. You can use it, even if you don't know any of the science behind it. Push a boulder off a cliff onto your enemy's head, and he's going to have a really bad day. You don't have to be Albert Einstein to be able to use it."

"Exactly right, Jenna," said Wyland, beaming. "Same with magic. We use it. We know it taps into science. We just don't know the science. And when we want to amplify our abilities or make our magic permanent, we've found a variety of crystals we can use to do this."

Zachary turned the language transformer in his hand, inspecting the purple crystal carefully. Finally he looked at Jenna, shrugged, and stuck it in his pocket as instructed. "I get how you can do magic without knowing any science—I mean, assuming there really is such a thing as magic. But wouldn't your magic be even stronger if you *did* know science? I mean—"

"Enough!" shouted Hirth. He scowled even more deeply at the two humans, which Zachary wouldn't have thought possible. "You are now done asking stupid questions, and *we* are now done answering them." When he said the word "we" he glared at his companion, as though his message was for Wyland's benefit as much as for the humans. "You need to proceed quickly. You have little time."

"Little time for what?" asked Jenna, realizing she didn't have to look away quite as often anymore. Maybe she and Zack were becoming used to these men's repulsive and unsettling appearance.

"You have to get moving," said Hirth impatiently. "I hope you're not upset that I almost hit you with my ground vehicle. We expected you to land a little farther down the road."

"You expected us?" asked Zachary.

"Well of course we did."

"Are you here to welcome us?" asked Jenna hopefully.

Wyland smiled and nodded, but Hirth looked as though he had just sucked on a lemon. "Welcome you?" he repeated nastily. "Definitely not! And for very good reason," he continued with brutal honesty. "Because you are *not* welcome here. I am here to usher you on your way—and away from here—as quickly as I can. Frankly, your kind make us nervous, not to mention a little nauseated."

"I don't understand," said Zachary.

The man frowned. "It should be obvious. Your kind are too feeble and unimaginative to use magic, as I've already said. In addition, you're covered in hideous, opaque skin, and we can't see anything inside of you. Disgusting!" declared the man. "We're a very straightforward, aboveboard people. But we've found your kind to be nearly impossible to understand; devious and confusing. And we don't trust you. How can you trust a person when you can't see what's inside him?"

"You can trust *us*," said Jenna innocently.

"It doesn't matter if we can or can't," snapped Hirth. "What matters is getting you on your way as soon as possible. You're trying to find your parents, correct?"

Their eyes widened. "How do you know that?" said Jenna.

"We don't have time for any more idle chatter," said Hirth. "I can direct you to one of two portals. You tell me which one. Option one: the one that your parents took. Option two: a portal that will lead you to your parents much more quickly."

Zachary's eyes widened. Hirth seemed to know exactly what was going on. His parents hadn't had any luck getting a native to share information with them. But before leaving this world, Zachary was determined to question this man in depth until he got some answers.

"Well," snapped the man. "To which portal would you like to be directed?"

"What's the catch?" asked Zachary.

Hirth looked confused. "The catch? A *catch* is something you find on a gate, or something you do when someone throws you a ball. What does that have to do with my question?"

"I mean, the decision seems *too* obvious. Is there any reason why we wouldn't take the shortcut that you haven't told us about?"

"Shortcut? Who said anything about cutting? I was speaking about portals." Hirth shook his head. "This is why your kind can't be trusted. You always try to change the subject."

Both kids realized why they were having trouble communicating at the same time. The people of this world apparently only used the precise dictionary definition of each word. Their interpretation of language, just like their bodies, left nothing to the imagination. If they told this man he had *lost his mind*, the man would *look* for it, thinking it was really lost. They would have to be careful to phrase everything as literally as possible here or they would quickly get into trouble.

"I think I'm beginning to *catch* on," whispered Zachary in his sister's ear, grinning.

Despite the seriousness of the situation, Jenna couldn't help but laugh at her brother's joke.

Zachary turned back toward Hirth. "Let me try this again," he said carefully. "Is there any reason why we wouldn't want to take the portal that will get us to our parents the fastest?"

"Congratulations," said Hirth. "You've actually managed to ask a question that shows you have more intelligence than a tree. The answer is yes. That route is much more dangerous than the one your parents took."

It figures, thought Zachary. *Just great.* He scratched his head. "What do you think, Jenna?"

"I think we need to take the shortcut," she answered, pleased that he had asked for her opinion.

"Me too," said Zachary. "Can you tell us the nature of the added danger?" he asked.

"No," replied Hirth sharply. He looked at his watch. "And you had better decide quickly. You barely have enough time to make it to one of the portals before your Anchor Fungus begins its second stage of growth and you two become very ugly . . . fixtures . . . here on our world."

The shorter transparent man, Wyland, had been silent for some time, but he suddenly burst angrily to life. "Anchor fungus!" he shouted. "Hirth, you are not authorized for this."

Hirth shrugged. "Too late now," he said simply.

Wyland's eyes were burning with anger, but he said nothing more.

"Anchor Fungus?" said Zachary. "I'm afraid I'm not following you."

"Of course you're not *following* me, because I refuse to *lead* you. If you were listening, you'll remember that I said I would *direct* you to a portal, not that I would *lead* you there."

This guy must be a ton of fun at parties, thought Zachary. "What is Anchor Fungus?" he asked, trying to stay as literal as possible.

"Pull up your pant legs and see for yourselves."

The siblings did so, and the color drained from their faces. They each had fuzzy green patches around their ankles, growing even as they watched. It was truly revolting.

"*That* is Anchor Fungus," explained Hirth, as if it should have been obvious.

Both kids began clutching at their ankles, trying to rub, scratch, or pull the sickening growth from themselves. But it was useless. They couldn't remove even a tiny part of it.

"Nothing you can do will deter it," said Hirth. "Believe me, anything you could possibly try has been tried before. It's harmless to us, but I infected you with it exactly five minutes ago, when Wyland here was being far more friendly to you than you deserve." He glared crossly at his companion once again.

"The infection begins on the ankles," continued Hirth. "But it will spread. In exactly—" he glanced at his watch, "and I do mean exactly—forty-nine minutes, the fungus will complete the first phase of its growth. At that time it will send tendrils down into the ground, growing from your ankles at the rate of several inches every few seconds. The tendrils can penetrate anything, so it will not help you to be standing on concrete. If you have not stepped through one of the portals, forty-nine minutes from now, the fungus will anchor you to the ground and then gradually wrap around your entire body."

Jenna and Zachary's faces curled up in horror.

"You will remain the unwanted guests of this world," continued the man with disdain. "Permanently."

CHAPTER SEVEN

Escape Route

The two humans shrank back in revulsion. What a horrible, horrible way to go.

As if reading their thoughts, Hirth continued. "It won't kill you, that's the worst part. It feeds off energy produced by your bodies. It will keep you alive for a long, long time, exposing us to your repulsiveness all the while."

Zachary gulped. "What happens to the fungus if we reach a portal before it, ah . . . roots?"

"Nothing happens to it if you *reach* a portal before then. If you go *through* a portal before then and leave Orum, it will die instantly and you will suffer no after effects."

"Why would you do this to us?" demanded Jenna in horror.

"I want you off Orum as soon as possible," replied Hirth. "And yet you seemed to be in no hurry to get anywhere. I believe that you will now be more . . . motivated . . . to leave."

"No kidding," snapped Zachary bitterly. "So tell us how to get to the portal. We choose the one that will get us to our parents faster."

"Follow me," said Hirth, and without another look behind him made his way to the car he had been driving, while the kids and Wyland followed.

"You don't have time to make it to a portal on foot," said Hirth. He gestured to the car. "So take this ground vehicle we were using. The citizens of Orum all share the few vehicles we have, since nobody really needs one."

"Why don't you need them?" said Jenna. "What? Are you saying that you can just travel, you know . . . magically . . . wherever you want?"

"That is correct," said Hirth.

"*Right*," said Zachary skeptically. "Then why don't you just transport us to the portal now and save some time?"

"Because you're uninvited visitors to our world. You're lucky I'm letting you use the ground vehicle."

"If you don't need them," said Jenna. "Why do you *have* them?"

"Using magic too often can be tiring," replied Wyland. "So we don't use it for everything. We have imbued some devices, like ground vehicles, with magic crystals, so we don't have to always make efforts of our own. For many trips, a ground vehicle works just fine."

Sure it does, thought Zachary in disbelief, but he decided not to challenge them any further. "Okay. Whatever you say." He shook his head. "But here's the problem. Jenna and I haven't learned how to drive yet."

"Don't be stupid," snapped Hirth. "This ground vehicle responds to verbal commands from whoever is inside. Just tell it what you want it to do and always stay in the right lane."

Zachary raised his eyebrows but said nothing. He quickly opened the door and settled into the driver's seat while Jenna sat beside him.

Zachary cleared his throat. "Lower window," he said tentatively, wondering if Hirth was trying to make a fool of him, but the car carried out his command immediately.

He nodded approvingly at the transparent man through the open window. Hirth was still repulsive, but Zachary could now look at him for long periods of time without looking away. And while Wyland looked almost exactly like Hirth, his more friendly nature somehow made his appearance slightly easier to take.

"Okay. Direct us to the portal," said Zachary. He was going to add, "and we'll get out of your hair," when he decided not to. Hirth would just tell him that they were never *in* his hair.

Hirth came forward, shoved a pad of paper and a pen into Zachary's hand, and then quickly retreated to a tolerable distance once again. "Write this down," he ordered. "Continue on the road you're now on. Six miles from here it will branch into five different roads, numbered one through five. At the branch point you'll find a wooden beam, sticking out from a booth. The beam is twenty yards due west of an old-fashioned well, so you shouldn't have any trouble finding it. On this wooden beam you'll find a ping-pong ball."

"Did you say a ping-pong ball?" said Jenna in disbelief.

"Yes I did. You really should pay closer attention," scolded Hirth once again. "Where was I? Oh yes. Inside the ball you'll find a small piece of paper with the number of the road you'll need to take."

"Why don't you just tell us the road we need to take *now*?" asked Jenna from the passenger's seat. Directions inside a ping-pong ball? It reminded her of a fortune cookie. It seemed more than just a little odd.

"Because the local portal appears in one of five locations each day, but we never know which one. Once we know, this information is imbedded in the ball, which is then placed on the wooden beam—using magic, of course. That's just how it's done. Since your imagination is too limited to even *use* magic, I would suggest not spending time criticizing how we do things here. I don't *have* to be this nice," he finished.

This nice? thought Jenna. Was he kidding?

But of course he wasn't, she realized. He wasn't the type to *ever* kid—about anything.

"Yeah," she said sarcastically. "You've been *super* friendly. I've never met anyone with a bigger, um— "

she hesitated and made a show of staring at the throbbing organ beating away inside Hirth's chest. "Heart," she finished.

"Should I go on or do you want to waste more time asking questions?"

"Go on, go on," said Jenna unhappily.

"One of the five roads has a very low bridge—an overpass—running over it that is too low for this vehicle to pass beneath. If this happens to be the road to which the ball directs you, lower the vehicle's airplane and continue."

The vehicle's airplane? Both listeners were confused but knew better than to interrupt. Not with the fungus growing stronger every second. Zachary continued scribbling everything the man said furiously on the pad.

"Whichever of the five roads the message in the ball directs you to, the portal will be inside a building you'll find on the right side of the road, eight miles from the branch-point. The door responds to verbal commands, just like the ground vehicle. When you have said today's correct passwords the door will open automatically. The passwords needed to enter the building are the four words you can make, without any rearrangements, from the letters that you find in there."

Hirth stopped abruptly. "That's all. Now get going and get off our world. This has been most unpleasant."

"But wait," said Zachary, totally confused about the passwords. "I don't understand what you mean by— "

"I said that's all!" interrupted Hirth with finality. "I've told you everything you need to know." He handed Zachary a watch. "You now have forty-two minutes," he announced. "Now leave!"

Zachary pulled up his pant leg and noted uneasily that the fungus had been making obvious progress even in the short time since he had last looked. He took a deep breath. "Before we go, can you tell us what happened to our parents? What this is all about?"

Hirth blinked in disbelief. "Have I failed to make myself understood? Even if you leave immediately you'll be fortunate to escape Orum in time. You can't afford to waste a single second."

"Since we're the ones infected, why don't you let us worry about that," insisted Zachary. His parents had reported failing to learn what was happening to them. If he and his sister were to have any chance of staying alive and rescuing them, they would have to learn exactly what they were up against, no matter what the cost.

"Look," said Zachary. "*You* want us off your world and *we* want us off your world. So tell us what you know really fast and we'll leave. Everyone will be happy."

Hirth folded his arms against his repulsive chest with an expression that made it clear he would not say a single additional word to the two humans.

"We really can't help you," said Wyland, and unlike the bitter tone of his taller companion, his tone was almost apologetic. "But I can tell you this: your parents are still alive. And there is a small chance you can find them. And finally, there is an explanation for all of this."

"Once again, Wyland," snapped Hirth, "You are wasting time. These beings are far too stupid and unimaginative to have any hope of finding their parents."

Zachary's hands balled up into fists. Hirth thought he was *so* superior. It was *maddening*. Hirth was so . . . arrogant. Was this how Zachary came across to others? It was a troubling thought. No, he decided. He may have been confident, but he was friendly and cheerful most of the time. This Hirth was rude and unpleasant at all times.

"We'll see who is stupid and unimaginative!" hissed Zachary, unable to contain his rage any longer. "If there is a way to find them, we'll figure it out," he insisted. "I promise you that."

"No," said Hirth. "You will flunk miserably." He turned to Wyland. "Let's go," he said.

Zachary still wasn't ready to give up. Why wouldn't the man tell them what he knew? Or let Wyland tell them? What was the big secret? Their parents had obviously run into the same problem, having talked to numerous aliens, most likely with the help of a language transformer, without getting any answers. "Can you at least tell us—"

"Enough!" barked Hirth. "This conversation is over." With that, he turned and strode briskly away, pulling his reluctant companion with him.

Zachary's face turned red with fury but he knew they would get nothing further from this man and they couldn't afford to waste another second. "Go forward along this road as fast as possible," he said quickly to the car. It immediately began moving forward. Driving a voice-controlled car would have been very cool if not for the horrible circumstances they were in.

"Do you know what I liked about Hirth?" asked Jenna.

Zachary shook his head. "No, what?"

"Absolutely nothing," she said impishly. "He was pretty much a complete and total jerk."

Zachary smiled. At least Jenna had kept her sense of humor, despite being infected with a fungus that would soon root them in the ground of this world forever.

After driving for a few minutes they saw a sharp bend in the road ahead. "Reduce speed to thirty miles per hour," said Zachary hurriedly, knowing they'd never make the turn at their current speed. The car began slowing immediately.

The road beyond the bend was hidden from view by a large farmhouse. As they approached the bend another car shot around it from the opposite direction and came into view.

The car was in their lane. And it was headed straight for them.

Zachary and Jenna had only an instant to brace themselves for a bone-crushing impact they could do nothing to avoid.

CHAPTER EIGHT

Hole in One

With an ear-piercing screech of its tires the oncoming car swerved violently to their left, avoiding a head-on collision by mere centimeters and shattering their side mirror as it whistled by.

"Stupid Hog!" shouted the transparent driver to Zachary through an open window as he passed.

Zachary's blood boiled in rage. This reckless driver had been in *his* lane, not the other way around. This maniac had almost killed them all by not controlling his car and he had the nerve to call *Zachary* a stupid hog.

Zachary had had more than enough of these transparent people. He stuck his head out of the window. But just as he opened his mouth to yell, "Reckless idiot!" at the other driver at the top of his lungs, he heard Jenna beside him yell, "*Immediate stop!*" as loudly as she could.

The car slammed on its breaks to carry out Jenna's order and both passengers were thrown into their seatbelts and shoulder restraints with great force.

And not a moment too soon.

As they rounded the bend a massive hog, the size of a large hippo, appeared in front of them, completely blocking the road. It was just as transparent—and disgusting—as the men they had met. But as hard as the car was braking they were still traveling too fast.

The car continued screeching to a halt, so close now that the monstrous pig filled up the entire windshield.

And then, miraculously, the car stopped. Just inches from the gigantic hog.

The disgustingly transparent animal considered them, bored, gave them a snort, and then lazily continued on its way across the street.

If Jenna hadn't called a stop when she did they would have definitely crashed into the massive pig, possibly killing them, certainly destroying the car and any chance they had to leave this world before falling victim to the Anchor Fungus.

"How did you know to stop the car?" said Zachary, his heart still racing madly.

"Well," said Jenna, "the people here are very literal, right? So when the driver yelled out, *stupid hog*, I realized he wasn't trying to insult you. He was trying to *warn* you. Warn you that a *stupid hog* had wandered into the road. That's why the driver was in our lane—he had to swerve to avoid the hog."

Zachary whistled. That was quick thinking on Jenna's part. He had let his temper get the best of him—and not for the first time. But on this journey, unlike back at home, his life could well depend upon his ability to control this temper.

As they started to move again, Zachary took one last look at the animal they had almost hit. "I've heard of road hogs before," he joked, "but I always thought that this was just a figure of speech." He turned to his sister. "Good job, Jenna. See, I knew you might come in handy. Let this be a valuable lesson for you: never doubt your brother."

Jenna rolled her eyes, but it did feel great to have actually been a help, especially after Zack had saved her from getting hit by Hirth's car. Was the Omega-wave generator working? She did feel stronger and her thoughts did seem to be coming faster and more clearly. In fact, she felt terrific. What a discovery her parents had made. If only they could get back home so they could give it to the world.

A few minutes later they came to the branch-point in the road, just as Hirth had said. They were making good time. Zachary estimated that they would get to the portal with five or ten minutes to spare.

They quickly spotted the booth the man had told them about, sitting near an old-fashioned red brick well, complete with a wood bucket and crank, as promised. Protruding from the booth, about three feet off the ground, was a beam of wood with a small indentation at the end. A ping-pong ball was sitting in the indentation. It was on Jenna's side.

Zachary had the car park itself beside the ball so his sister could grab it without getting out. Jenna reached out eagerly for the ball, but before her fingers had closed around it her hand brushed against it and knocked it from its perch.

The ball bounced, almost falling into the well, which would have been disastrous. Jenna bolted from the car after it. It began rolling down a slight incline by the side of the street. She almost had it. Almost. She reached.

The ball disappeared down a hole.

"No!" she shrieked. *It couldn't be.*

She had been so close. She knelt down to examine the hole and Zachary joined her a second later. What kind of hole was this and what could it possibly be doing here? It was concrete, as big around as a soda can, and it went straight down for fifteen or twenty feet. The odds against the ball rolling into this small opening were astronomical.

"How could I be so clumsy?" she groaned.

Zachary frowned deeply. They were in big trouble. How was it possible for their luck to be this bad? They sat by the hole and stared down at the ball resting at the bottom, far below, mocking them. It was the ultimate torture. The ball was right under their noses, but it might as well have been a thousand miles away.

And without the information inside the ball, they were as good as fungus food.

CHAPTER NINE

Blocked

Zachary was furious with the universe for playing such a dirty trick on them. He felt like screaming at the top of his lungs, but instead forced himself to take several deep breaths, determined not to lose his temper again like he had in the car. He looked at the watch Hirth had given him. "We'd better go, Jen. We still might get lucky and guess the right road. We have a one in five chance," he said with as much hope as he could manage.

Jenna had never felt so bad. Maybe she deserved to be turned into a human fungus. She had helped them avoid the giant hog, but now she had gone and pulled an idiotic move like fumbling the ping-pong ball. They were going to suffer a fate worse than death and it was all her fault. She lowered her head and began to sob. All the fear and emotion she had kept bottled up came out at once. The tears cascaded down her face and onto the pavement.

Zachary felt bad for his sister. Given what had happened they were working together as a team, but even when they were at each other's throats he hated to see Jenna so upset that she cried. Maybe he could say something to help.

"It's okay, Jen," he said gently, watching the tears fall from her face.

Drip. Drip. Drip.

"It wasn't your fault. I mean, yeah, you were super clumsy and all, but it was just really bad luck that the ball fell into that tiny opening."

His attempt to comfort her didn't help. In fact, if anything her sobbing got stronger. He replayed what he had said in his mind. Maybe he should have left out the "yeah, you were super clumsy," part. That probably wasn't helpful. He had finally found something he stunk at: being supportive. Lifting his sister up rather than tearing her down.

Drip-drip. Drip-drip. Drip-drip.

He shook his head helplessly. Jenna's tears were falling onto the pavement even faster now, forming a tiny stream that inched forward toward the hated hole.

Zachary bolted upright.

Toward the hole.

"That's it!" he shouted. "Jen, you've done it! We still have a chance." Without waiting for a response he rose and raced over to the well, turning the crank furiously to lower the bucket. He was rewarded seconds later by the sound of the bucket splashing down far below.

"Yessss!" he shouted happily. The well had plenty of water. He waited for the bucket to fill and then hurriedly cranked it back up.

Jenna stopped crying and watched in confusion as her brother raced around like a lunatic. He sprinted back carrying the bucket, ignoring the water splashing him as he ran. He knelt down and gently began pouring the water into the concrete hole.

And then Jenna understood. *Of course.*

Just as Zachary had hoped, the ball floated on top of the rising column of water. He continued pouring slowly as the ball rose, closer and closer to the top.

"It's a good thing you're so weak and emotional," he said to his sister. "Because your crying gave me the idea."

Jenna glared at him and shook her head.

"What?" he said defensively. "I was just telling you that you helped us. You're not stupid enough to take that the wrong way, are you?"

Right after these words left his mouth, Zachary cursed himself. Wow, beating his sister down had become such a reflex that he could barely control himself. And until their discussion before leaving home, he wouldn't have even realized he was doing it.

While he had been thinking, he continued to pour water into the hole, and the ball finally floated to the very top, easily accessible to their fingers. Zachary grabbed it and anxiously broke it open. Inside was a small piece of paper with the number three written on it.

They ran to the car and quickly instructed it to take road three at maximum speed. Zachary looked at his watch. "I think we're still going to make it."

Jenna couldn't have been more relieved. By mishandling the ball she had nearly cost them everything. "Any idea of what this is all about?" she asked her brother. If she could help him figure things out, even in a small way, maybe she could redeem herself.

Zachary shook his head.

"How did Hirth and Wyland know we were looking for Mom and Dad?" said Jenna.

"I don't know," replied Zachary. "Maybe they saw them come through the portal, too. Maybe when they saw *us*, they just figured the adult humans must have been our parents."

"Maybe," said Jenna. "But they were pretty certain. Maybe they know there's a portal in the kitchen of the Lane family."

Zachary frowned. Neither explanation was very good. "Maybe we should start at the beginning. What do we know? We know a portal appeared and swallowed Mom and Dad. Since we haven't exactly heard about portals before, we have to assume this hasn't ever happened on Earth."

"Or at least not very often."

"Right. So the first question is, what caused it to appear? It could just be some weird natural event that we don't know about that happens when conditions are just right. Like a tornado. Nobody causes it; it just happens."

"Maybe. But I doubt it. I think this one was created on purpose."

Zachary frowned. "You're probably right. I mean, what are the odds that it would appear exactly underneath Mom and Dad? A billion to one?"

"You don't think Dad had something to do with this, do you?" said Jenna. Their father worked on some far-out stuff like black holes and ten-dimensional space.

Zachary thought about it for a second. "Nah," he said. "I asked him once if he thought we'd ever invent a way to travel between worlds without using a spaceship. He said that with or without a spaceship, it would be a very long time before we figured out how to travel such great distances—if ever. And if he *was* responsible, he would have told us—I mean he would have had the Mimic Bird tell us—so we'd know what we were up against."

"Yeah, you're right." She scratched her head. "Besides, this world seems to have had a lot of these portals for a long time, and Dad couldn't have been responsible for *them*." Jenna paused. "But if someone did create the portal on purpose, maybe their goal was to get Mom and Dad. Maybe they were kidnapped."

"I don't think so," said Zachary. "They didn't say they were prisoners."

"Maybe whoever did this knew Mom and Dad could never get back to Earth. Maybe that was the plan. Maybe it was a jealous physicist who wanted Dad out of the way, or maybe even a chemist who wanted Mom out of the way." Jenna sighed, realizing how silly she must be sounding and then, grinning broadly, added, "Or maybe it was the intergalactic bad-cooking police finally catching up to Mom."

A smile flashed across Zachary's face. "One thing's for sure; we don't have nearly enough information to answer any of these questions . . . yet. Let's just hope we can learn more on the next world."

Jenna nudged her brother who hadn't been watching the road. "Zack, about getting to the next world—I think we have another problem."

Zachary looked up and groaned.

What incredibly bad luck. Again.

They were rapidly approaching the lowest concrete overpass he had ever seen. "I can't believe it. The transparent man warned us about this. The car won't fit under it. Why would anyone build one so low over the road?" he complained. "It just doesn't make sense."

They pulled up until they were just in front of the overpass. Zachary had the car inch forward towards it. Closer. Closer. Maybe the car would be able to squeeze under, after all. They were going to make it.

THUNK. The top of the car connected firmly with the overpass and the car stopped. They couldn't go under it, and there was no way around it, either. *Just great*.

"Now what?" said Jenna. If they couldn't get through, they had no chance to make it to the portal in time. And they weren't about to get help. They hadn't seen a single car on the road since the hog incident. Maybe the residents of Orum really *didn't* use cars.

Zachary consulted his pad. "Hirth told us to *lower the vehicle's airplane* if we came across this overpass. Those were his exact words."

They searched the car and trunk as thoroughly as possible, but didn't find anything, let alone an airplane.

"Why would he tell us to lower the car's airplane, if there is no airplane?" said Jenna.

Her brother shrugged. "I don't know," he said. "It looks like we're on our own. We'd better figure out *something*."

Zachary jumped out of the car and climbed onto its roof to examine the situation. Jenna joined him. The top of the car was about two inches too high to make it under the insanely low bridge. The car frame was solid steel and the bridge was solid concrete.

"Let's try jumping up and down," suggested Jenna. "Maybe we can cave the roof in enough to get through."

"Okay," said Zachary, jumping as high as he could and trying to slam his feet into the roof as hard as possible. Jenna joined him. After about a minute of trying, however, the roof wasn't so much as scratched. It was hopeless.

They got back into the car. "We're going to have to try to *ram* it through," said Zachary.

"Ram it? It's far too solid. We'll never make it—and we'll probably kill ourselves."

"What's our other choice?" said Zachary. "Becoming human fungus?"

Jenna grimaced. "Well, when you put it *that* way . . . "

They backed the car up about thirty yards, tightened their seatbelts and shoulder harnesses, and ordered the car to drive full speed ahead. As the car accelerated they closed their eyes. In another second it would be over. One way or another.

With a terrible screech the top of the car hit the overpass, slamming its two passengers into their belts with bone-jarring force before coming to a complete stop an instant later. Fortunately for them the seatbelts and the car were well made and they escaped serious injury. The front part of the roof had been caved in by the impact, but not enough. The car had only made it halfway and was now wedged tightly under the bridge.

Their situation had been hopeless before.

Now it was far worse.

CHAPTER TEN

Tendrils

Zachary brought down his fist, hammer-like, on the steering wheel. "That's it. We're finished. We're trapped like a cork. How could our luck be so bad! First the ping-pong ball, and now this. And the only instructions we get from Mr. See-Through involve an imaginary airplane."

Jenna had an odd feeling there was something she had missed. The Omega waves coming from the generator were working their magic and she was thinking quite clearly. She closed her eyes, deep in concentration. "Wait a minute," she said. "Would they have called an airplane an airplane?"

"What are you talking about?"

"Would Hirth and Wyland have used the word *airplane* to describe an airplane? Remember they kept calling the car a g*round vehicle*. If they were talking about what we call an airplane they would have called it an *air vehicle*. Hirth must have meant something else."

"You're probably right," agreed Zachary. "But what else could he have meant?"

Jenna concentrated. "Maybe he meant it to be two words, not one. Air and Plane. *Lower the vehicle's Air Plane*."

"And a plane is a level in geometry. So he might have meant, '*Lower the vehicle's air level*'."

Jenna frowned. "But that still doesn't help us."

Zachary's eyes widened. "Yes it does!" he said excitedly. "A car has two horizontal levels, or *planes*. One is its roof. We tried to lower that. But the other level . . . the other level is where the body of the car sits on its tires. *Its tires, Jen!* And tires are filled with air! *The Air Plane.* And we *can* lower that."

"That has to be it!" said Jenna.

Wasting no more time they jumped from the car and rapidly let out most of the air from the tires. The car sank several inches, enough to allow them to move slowly forward under the low overpass. Moments later they were beyond it and driving ahead at full speed. The drive was less comfortable with a smashed roof and severely deflated tires, but that was the least of their worries.

Zachary glanced nervously at the watch once again and fought back panic. They had wasted considerable time getting beyond the overpass.

"Hirth told us that the passwords needed to enter the building," he said, consulting the notepad, "*were the four words you can make, without any rearrangements, from the letters that you find in there.*"

"So let me get this straight. We need to find letters inside this building and then make four words using them?"

"Right. And these four words will open the door."

Jenna scratched her head. "But if we can't open the door without the four words, how do we find the letters inside in the first place?"

"Good question. It's like telling us the key to a locked building is *inside* the building. How does that help us?"

"Maybe the building's made of glass," said Jenna. "Maybe it's just as see-through as the people. Then we'd be able to see the letters."

"I sure hope you're right," said Zachary.

They rounded a corner and a building about the size of a small house came into view. Inside this distant building was the portal—their ticket off this bizarre world.

As they neared the building Zachary examined the fungus growing around his ankles once again. He was overcome by a momentary wave of nausea at the sight of it. It was now several inches thick and it had sprouted tiny buds: buds that would soon form vines to tether him to the ground.

They stopped the car right next to a large door at the front of the structure. Zachary's heart fell as he realized Jenna's guess had been wrong. The building was a perfect cube with no glass, no windows, and no way to see inside. So much for that theory. Now what?

They jumped out of the car and tried the large door, the building's only entrance. It was solid steel and had to be at least a foot thick. It didn't even budge.

Suddenly, the watch Hirth had given them started to beep loudly. The shrill tone, repeated over and over again, could only mean one thing—their time was up. Sure enough, small, green tendrils began slithering out from under their pant legs, growing snakelike toward the ground. They both gasped in horror. It was happening. Just as Hirth had said it would.

"*Climb on top of the car!*" yelled Zachary, grabbing the note pad and scampering on top of the roof. "*Hurry!* It'll take the vines longer to reach the ground. At least it will buy us some more time."

Jenna quickly joined him on the car's roof as the vines continued their terrible growth downward. They had less than a minute to come up with the passwords.

And they were completely out of ideas.

CHAPTER ELEVEN

The Forest World

Zachary watched in horror from his position on top of the car as the rope-like fingers continued to grow eagerly downward from his ankles, hungrily searching for the ground. He reached down and tried to break one of the vines but it was incredibly strong and easily resisted his efforts.

Jenna had a sudden inspiration. "Any way to take what he told us more literally?" she said hurriedly.

"I don't know. I'll try," said Zachary, scanning Hirth's instructions once again. But he couldn't concentrate. Not with the fungus snaking its way toward the ground. *He had to find a way to focus.* He shook his head vigorously, as if to clear it, and looked down at the pad.

The passwords to get into the building are the four words you can make, without any rearrangements, from the letters that you find in there.

From the letters that you find in there. Don't assume anything about meaning. *From the letters that you find in there. Concentrate*, he ordered himself.

Wait. What if *there* didn't refer to the building. He and Jenna had made that assumption. What if Hirth was just referring to the word, T-H-E-R-E. Were there four words that could be made, without rearranging any letters, from the letters found in the word THERE?

He glanced down. The tendrils were now just inches from the ground and closing quickly. He looked back at the pad. And he saw the four words.

THEre, t**HERE**, t**HE**re, t**HER**e

He had it. The vines were just entering the ground. Was he too late?

"THE, HERE, HE, HER," he shouted at the door.

There was a loud click and the door began to slowly open. Several tendrils had now reached the ground and were tunneling into the earth.

"You did it!" shouted Jenna excitedly. "How?"

"I'll explain later. Get ready."

The door had opened just enough for them to squeeze through. Their only hope now was that the portal was just inside the door rather than deep inside the building.

It was. Finally, some good luck.

The familiar visual distortion of the portal greeted their eyes less than a foot from the door. They gathered up the few tendrils that had begun to burrow into the ground and yanked as hard as they could. The tendrils held.

Zachary grabbed his sister's hand. "Dive for it!" he shouted, praying there was enough slack in the vines for them to make it through.

Together they dived off the car and through the door, aiming for the portal, screaming as they shot through the air. The slack in the vines around their ankles was quickly taken up as they flew. Would there be enough, or would the vine snap them back before they reached their goal?

"Ahhhhhhhh" they both yelled in one continuous scream, squeezing their eyes shut tightly.

And then they hit the portal, dead center—and at the same instant felt a backward jerk from the now taut vines. Had they made it through in time?

Jenna opened her eyes.

They were through. *They had done it*.

Although they had dived through the portal headfirst, they had somehow arrived comfortably on their feet as they had after entering the portal in their kitchen.

The fungus that had gone through with them was writhing rapidly and turning brown. Within seconds it stopped moving and fell from around their ankles.

"We did it!" shouted Jenna joyfully. They inspected themselves carefully for any trace of fungus or injury and found none.

Zachary nodded, letting out a long, thankful breath. "Did we ever," he said. "Talk about close calls."

They were standing in the middle of a lush forest filled with trees that made the largest trees on Earth look like miniatures. The massive trunks were as big around as houses and the trees reached hundreds of feet into the air, branching extensively.

The forest was mostly green, and if not for the sheer size and density of the trees, it might have passed for an exotic jungle on Earth. The many leaves formed a shady canopy, keeping the forest below shielded from the extreme brightness and heat of the sun, providing a cool, pleasant climate. The forest floor was thick with wild flowers of every color along with mushrooms, mosses, and lush grasses. The air was crisp and fresh and filled with the faint scent of flowers and other living things that, while unlike anything they had smelled before, was quite pleasant.

"This is my kind of place," said Zachary.

"Incredible," whispered his sister in agreement.

Just seconds before they had been battling for their lives on top of a car in the middle of sprawling farmland and now—in the blink of an eye—they were standing in a lush forest on some other world, as if the transparent man's world had never existed. These portals were going to take some getting used to.

Jenna looked at her brother quizzically. "But how'd you do it? How'd you figure out the passwords?"

Zachary told her. Her idea to take Hirth's instructions literally had been the key.

"Great job," she said in admiration. "Only next time," she added playfully, "can you cut our escape a little closer? You know, just to make it more exciting. I mean, you probably could have waited at least another billionth of a second."

Zachary laughed.

"I think we make a pretty good team," said Jenna happily.

"We make a *great* team. I'm proud of us. I'm proud of *you*. You really came through, Jenna."

His sister beamed.

That was better, thought Zachary. This time he had managed to give Jenna an actual compliment without also insulting her at the same time. If only he could do this when she was sobbing uncontrollably, he might be on to something.

"Unfortunately," he said grimly, "not to rain on our parade or anything." He could almost hear Hirth telling him that it *was not* raining and there was *no* parade. "But even though we feel like we conquered the universe, all we've really done is manage to stay alive for a single hour in here. *A single hour*."

Jenna nodded. He was right. It was a sobering thought. Their mom and dad had been searching for a way home for *months*.

"And remember," said Zachary as if reading her mind. "The path we're now on is supposedly more dangerous than the one Mom and Dad took."

"Zack, that's not raining on our parade. That's hitting our parade with a nuclear bomb."

"Sorry. I just want to make sure we stay on guard."

"Consider me on guard," she said.

He was right, of course. But it sure was hard to believe this magnificent place was dangerous. Jenna rested against a thick branch of a tree whose trunk was thirty yards distant. Its branches, like the one on which Jenna leaned, started only a few feet off the ground and rose with the tree to a point higher than she could follow with her eyes. Thick vines hung down limply from the higher regions.

They tilted their heads back and gazed in awe at the magnificent world above them for several minutes. Zachary was so enthralled he was beginning to wonder if the danger of this place was that he would never want to leave it.

Finally, Jenna broke the long silence. "So . . . do we have a plan?"

Zachary shrugged. "Not really. I guess we just wander around until we either run into someone who can help us or we run into another portal."

Jenna gritted her teeth. "So our plan is to get lucky?"

"Kind of. Mr. Ugly back on Orum said Mom and Dad were never on this world. It's just a shortcut to get to them. So we should jump off as soon as we can."

"How do we know we'll find a portal?"

"We don't. But Hirth was sure this would be a quicker way to get to Mom and Dad. So there must be a portal around here somewhere."

"I sure hope you're . . ."

CRACK! The sound reverberated through the forest, interrupting her, followed by a muffled wail. It had come from the branches directly above them.

Startled, they looked up.

Fifty feet directly above, a strange, armored creature was hanging over them menacingly.

CHAPTER TWELVE

The Terrible Grull

What in the world? Was this creature in an attacking position? Was it preparing to pounce?

After the first moment of surprise the pieces started to fall into place. It was an alien: judging from appearances, a boy, about the same age as Zachary. Not human, but human-like. The alien was covered with thick, gray, armored plates that were a part of his body, like an armadillo or turtle. His lower body and legs were massive, rippling with strength, and while the boy was only as tall as Jenna, he easily weighed three times as much.

And he was in big trouble.

The armored alien wasn't preparing to attack; he was about to fall out of the tree. He had been at the end of a branch that, thick as it was, had cracked under his weight. The end of the branch was now hanging straight down from the break point, still partially attached to the rest of the branch, and the alien was hugging it and hanging on for dear life. And he was slipping down, ever so slowly. Another five feet and he would slip off for good.

"*Hang on*," shouted Zachary at the top of his lungs. "*We're coming to help you.*"

They began climbing as quickly as they could, but it still took them several minutes to reach the boy's level in the tree. As they climbed the poor alien slipped several more feet and was grunting from the immense physical exertion.

"Hang on," said Zachary again as he reached the boy's level and took a quick survey. There were no branches that came closer to the struggling alien than fifteen yards, but he saw that he could swing from a vine, Tarzan-like, and reach him. Zachary grabbed a vine he thought would do the trick and yelled out, "I'm gonna swing over and try to land above you on the broken branch. Grab the vine and we can swing back together."

Jenna shook her head. "It's better if I go, Zack. I'm lighter."

"It's way too dangerous. There's no way I'm going to let you— "

"You know I'm right," she interrupted. "Besides, I'm not strong enough to push you out far enough to reach him. But you could push *me* there." She gripped the vine tightly. "We don't have time to argue about it."

Zachary frowned. She was right. The armored native had less than a minute before he would plummet to the ground. They had to act now.

"Hold on tight," said Zachary, shoving his sister toward the broken limb as hard as he could.

Jenna exploded outward in a long arc. When she neared the branch she reached out and hooked one arm around it while keeping her grip on the vine. "Hurry!" she grunted at the alien. "Grab the vine. I can't hold on much longer!"

The boy reached out and seized the vine just as Jenna lost her grip on the broken branch. They both swung wildly back, overshooting Jenna's starting point by a wide margin. Zachary caught the vine and slowed its wild swinging. Once it was stabilized over his sister's original perch, Jenna and the native lowered themselves to safety.

The alien rubbed his overworked arms, wincing. He turned to the humans in dismay. "Why did you do that?"

They looked at each other, puzzled.

"Why?" repeated Jenna in confusion. "Because it looked like you were in big trouble. We were trying to save your life."

"I *was* in big trouble," he replied. "And you *did* save my life. But I still don't understand. I'm not one of your people. You didn't know me. Why would you put yourself at risk to help me?"

"Because you needed help," was all that Jenna could think of to say.

"Very, very strange," said the boy, shaking his armored head.

He reached out and pressed gently on Zachary's stomach. "You're softbodied *people*. I didn't know there was such a thing."

"We're not from here," offered Zachary, continuing to be amazed by the incredible performance of the language transformer crystal they had been given. As much as he still resisted the idea, maybe it *was* magical.

The armored native nodded. "That's obvious. I've never seen any creature here who would help a creature of another kind. You are very strange. But . . ." he paused as if at a loss for the right word. "Thanks. Thanks for saving my life."

"We're glad we could help," said Jenna.

"My name is Zachary, by the way," said Zachary, trying to be friendly. "And my sister here is named Jenna."

"I'm Tular," said the alien boy.

"Nice to meet you, Tular," said Jenna. She paused and then scratched her head. "Just out of curiosity, what were you doing up here anyway?"

The alien considered Jenna for several long seconds. "Well, to be honest," he said at last, lowering his head guiltily. "I was, um . . . spying on you."

"Spying?"

"Yeah. I had never seen anything like you before and I needed to learn how much of a threat you were—how dangerous. And then I overestimated the strength of a branch and it broke."

"Why would you think we were dangerous?" asked Jenna as the three of them began slowly working their way down the tree and back to the ground.

Tular looked confused. "You really don't have any idea what things are like here, do you?"

"I guess not," said Zachary.

"Well, for one, just about every living thing here is deadly," he said. "Let's get to the ground and I'll show you."

They climbed down in silence for another few minutes, at last making it to the ground. A beautiful grove of shiny blue flowers was growing only five yards away from where they had exited the tree. Each had a thick stalk that rose several feet to where an array of delicate blue petals folded back gracefully. The flowers had a bright, metallic sheen, making each look like an exquisite metal sculpture.

Jenna took a step toward the nearest flower. As she did so she watched, fascinated, as the petals slowly lifted from the sides of the flower's stalk, coming together to form a beautiful, pointed Tulip bulb.

"Can I pick one of these?" she asked

"Duck!" yelled the armored boy from behind her, grabbing her arm and pulling her down.

And not an instant too soon.

The plant she had been approaching, the stalk with the pointed metal flower on its end, had swiveled to face her and had blasted off from the earth, hurtling at fantastic speed like a missile right for her chest. It embedded itself like an arrow in a tree branch several feet behind her. If Tular hadn't pulled her down it would have embedded itself in her chest.

They watched in horror and fascination as the rope-like root attached to the stalk contracted, tugging at the stalk until the razor sharp, metal petals at its tip dislodged themselves from the tree. The root continued retracting into the ground, pulling the stalk and metallic flower with it back to its original position—ready to fire again.

"Okay. You've convinced me," said Tular, shaking his head in disbelief. "I wasn't sure you were telling the truth. These flowers are called Harpoon Tulips. And even the stupidest animal would know better than to approach one on *purpose*. You really don't have a clue, do you?"

They both shook their heads no.

"Then let me repeat," said Tular in exasperation. "*Everything* here is deadly. *Everything*."

"But why did it do that?" said Jenna. It just didn't seem right that such a stunningly beautiful flower would want to attack her like that.

Tular rolled his eyes. "It was hungry," he said, as if this were the dumbest question he had ever heard. "Once it impales a victim it digests them—from the inside out. I can't believe you were going to try to *pick* one," he added with the same expression of disbelief that a human would have shown had an alien wanted to pet a hungry crocodile.

Jenna shuddered at the thought of the horrendous fate she had narrowly missed. It clearly paid to become familiar with the native plant and animal life as quickly as possible. "What about that one?" she said, pointing to what looked like a large, metallic sunflower plant, bright orange in color. "That's dangerous, too?"

Tular nodded. "The Guillotine Flower. It's a lot like the Harpoon Tulip. Get too close and the flower launches the large, circular portion at its center, which becomes a flying disk. It has razor-sharp edges. And it aims for the neck."

As Tular was talking, a small bird, perhaps the size of Jenna's fist, flew in and hovered a few feet from her like a hummingbird would. It was soft pink in color, fuzzy, and adorably cute. She smiled at it. In the blink of an eye a lethal, pointed spike telescoped from the bird's forehead and it lunged toward her head. With blinding speed, Tular threw his armored hand in front of her and they heard the sound of metal on metal as the bird, mere inches away from drilling a hole in Jenna's forehead, collided with his hand and bounced off.

Unfazed, the bird stood up, shook itself, and then flew away, retreating farther into the forest.

"I wouldn't advise playing with a Swordbird, either," commented Tular.

Jenna gulped hard. "Good idea," she said. She turned to her brother. "As horrible as Hirth was, you can't say he didn't warn us this shortcut would be dangerous."

Zachary frowned. He was beginning to think that calling this world dangerous—even *extremely* danger-ous—was an understatement. He turned to face the ar-mored boy once again. "Can you tell us more about this place?"

"I'd be happy to," replied Tular. "Let's walk to my people's encampment while we talk," he suggested. "They'll definitely want to meet you two . . . because you're so different and also to thank you properly for saving me."

They set off through the forest, staying very close to Tular as he kept a watchful eye out so they wouldn't stumble into something dangerous.

"The animals here have developed a huge range of of-fensive and defensive strategies for survival," explained Tular. "About half of them have armor like I do—hard-body animals. Armor is a very handy defensive thing to have around here."

Jenna considered her two close calls with sharp, pointy objects. "*Very* handy," she agreed.

"About half the animals are softbodies," he contin-ued. "Like you. The softbodies don't carry heavy armor so they have lightning fast reflexes and incredible speed."

"That makes sense," said Jenna. "If you don't have armor protecting you, you'd better be able to run and dodge."

"Right. That's another reason I believe you when you say you don't belong here. I don't want to sound critical—and I am very grateful that you saved me—but you two are, *by far*, the slowest softbodies I've ever seen. You're even slower than *me*, and you don't have any armor."

"We're weak, too, at least compared to you," admitted Zachary. "It's pretty obvious we're not from here. We wouldn't have lasted five minutes here without you."

"What do you mean? It must have taken you days or weeks to travel here from your land. And you've obviously survived just fine." The armored alien shook his head. "Although I admit I have no idea how."

Zachary winced. "Yeah. About that . . ." he began, and then paused, searching for a good way to tell the alien how they had arrived. "About our journey here . . ."

"Would you mind waiting to tell of this until we're with my people?" asked Tular. "I'm sure it's an amazing tale, and they'll want to hear every word."

"Sure," said Zachary, knowing that Tular had no idea just how amazing of a tale it really was.

"Um . . . Tular," said Jenna. "You and your people don't have um . . . magical powers . . . by any chance, do you?"

Tular squinted. "You used a word that I've never heard before. I'm not sure what you're asking."

Jenna thought about how to respond. "I mean, none of you can float, can you? Or make things move with your mind? Or like, make things appear and disappear? Stuff like that."

"Is this a joke?" said Tular. "Of course not. No one can do things like that."

"Right," said Jenna. "You got me. It was a joke." She paused. "It's probably funnier where we come from," she mumbled.

They continued walking for half an hour. Every so often they were attacked by a different plant or animal. Tular was so accustomed to the dangers of his world that he deflected or avoided the attacks effortlessly, paying them no conscious attention. In fact, he continued with whatever he happened to be saying at the time without the slightest pause.

Zachary and Jenna learned that Tular and his people were called Krugs. They roamed the forest in clans of about a hundred, returning to a central camp. They relied on their heavy body armor, intelligence, vast knowledge of the forest, and skill at working together to survive. While their world had forced them to protect themselves against almost every other life form, they were innately gentle and generous by nature, and formed a very loving and peaceful community.

Finally, they arrived at Tular's encampment, which caused an immediate stir. Within seconds the entire encampment encircled them, listening spellbound while Tular described how the bizarre, softbody humans had rescued him. The crowd was enthralled, and Jenna and Zachary were showered with praise for saving a beloved member of their clan.

The two humans described their adventures from the time their parents had disappeared. The Krug had an insatiable curiosity and peppered them with question after question for nearly an hour. Despite their story being more fantastic than anything the Krug had ever heard, their honesty was never questioned.

Finally, the most ancient Krug elder called a halt to the proceedings. "Our honored guests have answered enough questions for now. We're sorry for getting so carried away. Hopefully, you can understand our curiosity."

"Absolutely," said Zachary. "In fact, we have some questions of our own."

A hush fell over the gathering. "We would be honored to answer any questions that we can."

"Thanks," said Zachary. "Have you or any other Krug clans ever come across softbody people like us?" he asked hopefully.

The elder shook his head. "None. Nothing even close."

Zachary nodded, not surprised given what Hirth had told them. "In that case, do you know where we can find a portal like the ones we've told you about? A portal to another world?" Zachary described their appearance as carefully as he could, including their strange shimmering.

As he described them, a stunned look came over the elder's face. "If you had asked this question two days ago," he said, "I would have told you that we have never heard of such a thing. But, remarkably, just yesterday we stumbled upon something that is exactly as you describe."

"Do you remember where it is?" asked Jenna.

"Absolutely. It's hard to forget something so incredibly strange. It is merely two miles distant, to the north. For the last two days it has appeared without fail. It appears and disappears in a regular pattern. It is present for four minutes, not present for five, present again for four, and so on—over and over and over again."

What a relief. The portals seemed to be staying close to them. "Would you mind if I talked to my sister in private for a few minutes?" said Zachary.

"Not at all," said the elder.

Zachary walked about ten yards away with his sister and huddled. "So what do you think?" he asked.

She shrugged. "I think we should go through it as soon as possible."

Zachary nodded. "I agree. We know Mom and Dad aren't here. And since these people don't know anything about portals, we probably won't learn anything from them that will help us." He paused in thought. "Before we leave, though, can you think of anything important this world and the first world have in common?"

"Why do you ask?"

"I don't know. Maybe if we could find some connection between worlds it would help us figure out what we've gotten ourselves into."

Jenna considered for several long seconds. "I can't think of anything," she said, shaking her head. "Hirth and Wyland seemed to know about everything—the portals, our family, what's really going on. This is a primitive forest world, and the people here know nothing about us or about portals. Or about magic." A troubled look crossed her face. "But this world feels real to me—the first one didn't for some reason: like it was a fantasy creation from the imagination of some twisted mental patient."

"It was incredibly bizarre, that's for sure," agreed Zachary.

"Do you think they could really use magic?" said Jenna.

Zachary shrugged. "I don't know. I mean, they didn't use any while we were there—they just talked about it. They could be putting us on."

"What about the language transformer?"

"Yeah, I thought the same thing. It does seem magical. But that doesn't mean it is. If someone visited Earth from a planet that didn't have technology, and we handed them a small rectangular device that could play movies, music, and let them talk to someone a thousand miles away, it would be easy to convince them it was magic."

Jenna nodded. A cell phone could do things that seemed magical when you really stopped to think about it.

"The weird part," continued Zachary, "is that controlling things with your mind *is* possible. One of Dad's scientist friends works in this area. You wear a headband and you can control a video game—with your *brain*. In a few years, magic and science really might be just about the same thing—just like Hirth and Wyland said."

"Wyland told us we could figure out what was going on," said Jenna. "But I don't see how. At least not with what we know now."

"I agree. It doesn't seem likely." Zachary paused, thinking about their encounter with the two transparent men. "Boy, Hirth and Wyland sure didn't seem to like each other."

"Hard to imagine how *anyone* could like Hirth," she said. "Do you think he sent the portal into our kitchen?"

Zachary frowned. "I thought about that, too. But for what reason? They can't stand humans—at least Hirth can't. He couldn't wait to get us off his planet. So why bring Mom and Dad to Orum just to hurry them off? What's in it for them?"

Zachary was right, thought Jenna. But even if the transparent men weren't behind it, they seemed to know who was. The fact that they refused to tell her or Zack was *infuriating*.

Jenna and her brother discussed their situation for a few minutes more and then rejoined the Krug.

"We'd be grateful if you could give us directions to the portal you told us about," said Zachary diplomatically to the Krug elder. "We'd very much like to go there as soon as possible."

The elder smiled graciously. "Of course. It's the least we can do after what you've done for us. Tular?" he called.

"I'd be happy to escort them," offered Tular, not needing to be asked.

"Thank you again for what you have done," said the elder. "I hope you find what you're looking for."

Within minutes they were on their way. This was turning out to be not so difficult, after all. It was true that this world was extremely dangerous, but they had been lucky to stumble upon Tular. Without him they wouldn't have stood a chance on this magnificent but deadly world. But now, in a very short time, they would be moving on to the next world, hopefully a step or two closer to their parents.

They were only seventy yards away from their destination when Tular gasped and bent down to examine the earth. He looked even more panic-stricken than he had been while hanging from the branch.

"What is it, Tular?" asked Jenna in concern.

Tular was shaking as he rose. "I can't believe it," he said. "A Grull track. A *Grull* is in the area. Worse still, it appears from these tracks that he's heading in the general direction of our encampment. If my people are surprised he could wipe out the entire camp singlehandedly. I have to go back immediately and warn them."

"A Grull?" said Jenna.

"Yes. The other intelligent species on our planet and our mortal enemy. They're the ultimate hunting machines: intelligent, cunning, and powerful. They're almost impossible to stop and unimaginably cruel. They love to terrorize others. To torture them and watch them suffer. They're pure evil."

Zachary gulped loudly. That didn't sound good. "But if they're so unstoppable, why aren't they running the planet?"

"There are very, very few of them anymore. They hate all life, even their own kind. They war with themselves continually and almost never have children. Their own evil and hatred will soon make them extinct. I haven't seen one in my entire life, but we're taught how to look out for them from early childhood and this is definitely one of their tracks."

Tular looked at them apologetically. "I'm so sorry, but I have to leave you. Just pass this tree trunk and make a hard left, and the portal should appear about forty yards in front of you. I'm sorry that I can't wait to see you through it and make sure you're safe."

"We understand," Jenna assured him. "Go back and warn your people."

"We'll be fine," added Zachary. "You've taught us enough that we should be able to survive for a few minutes until the portal comes. Thanks for everything."

"Thank *you*," said Tular gratefully as he began sprinting back the way they had come. "I will never forget you two."

Zachary and Jenna smiled and began walking the short distance to where the portal would appear. They passed the tree trunk and turned left, carefully avoiding a grove of Harpoon Tulips, and made it to the spot Tular had specified. And then two things happened at the same time.

The portal suddenly appeared from out of nowhere in front of them.

And they heard a booming growl, so fierce and thunderous, so terrible and hatred-filled, that it could only have come from one creature.

The Grull.

They sprinted back to the edge of the tree trunk forty yards from the portal and peered around it. Less than sixty yards away through the forest, Tular was flat on his back on the ground. And towering over him was the most terrible predator of all. The Grull bristled with raw strength and ferocity. It was ten feet tall and had the effortless strength of a Polar Bear. It was armored from head to toe and had dagger-like spikes protruding from its elbows and forehead. It had two mouths, one on top of the other, each filled with jagged, razor-sharp teeth, and also two sets of arms. One set of its arms ended in large, human-like hands, with lethal retractable claws. The other in sharp pincers, like the claws of a lobster, capable of cutting through bone and cartilage.

The monster stood calmly over a cowering Tular, cruel laughter booming from one of its mouths. "Going somewhere?" it taunted their friend, its voice so deep and loud that the words reverberated throughout the forest. "What's the rush? Stick around and let's have some fun."

Tular was no match for the Grull. He was clearly doomed, and with him his entire village.

"Scream at the top of your lungs," said Zachary to his sister. "We have to create a diversion. The Grull likes causing terror, so if we act terrified, it might leave Tular and come after us."

"If we *act* terrified," said Jenna. "It's not gonna take any acting on *my* part," she added as they left the cover provided by the tree trunk and began screaming as loudly as they could.

The Grull looked behind it and smiled with both mouths. "What in the world are these things?" it said to itself. It looked at Tular and then back at the softbody people. It had tortured plenty of Krug in its lifetime, but these creatures were something totally new. Its decision was obvious.

Moving with surprising quickness for a being so large it raced off after the softbodies, leaving Tular unattended.

"Go!" Zachary shouted to Tular at the top of his lungs just as the Grull took its first step away from him. "Warn your people. We'll be gone before it catches us," he finished, turning with Jenna and sprinting for the portal.

Tular sprang to his feet. He took one last look at his fleeing softbody friends before turning and running at full speed back to warn the encampment. These frail softbodies weren't even adults and they didn't have armor or great strength, but there was no questioning their bravery. Remarkable. They had earned an honored place in Krug history.

The humans continued their race to the portal, relieved that Tular was now running to safety. They had done it. The Grull had taken the bait and Tular had escaped. Now all they had to do was put a world between the Grull and themselves. They sprinted faster than they ever had in their lives.

Zachary threw a quick glance behind him as they ran. The Grull was rapidly gaining on them. Its speed was *incredible*. But it would still not catch them in time. Zachary concentrated on his running. The portal was only twenty-five yards ahead.

Twenty yards.

Fifteen.

The portal began to shrink.

No. Impossible. *It couldn't close now.*

Zachary was ten yards away. He was going to make it. It was shrinking but there would still be just enough of it present for them to dive through.

As he prepared to dive a horrible realization hit him: Jenna was three yards behind him. Because she was smaller and younger she wasn't as fast as he was. He would make it, but she would definitely not.

Zachary made his decision instantly. He could not go through without her. He slowed as the portal shrank into a single point and then disappeared, not to return for five full minutes. Five minutes they didn't have.

Their escape route gone, the faster Grull was on them in an instant, knocking them painfully to the ground with one of its mighty arms.

CHAPTER THIRTEEN

More Terrifying Than a Grull?

The Grull reached down and lifted both kids effortlessly into the air, one in each hand. It held them up to its face to inspect. They hung high above the ground, facing the monster, like dolls in the giant's awesome grip.

The Grull was holding a large, half eaten animal in one of its two massive claws. It had carried this bloody carcass effortlessly while it had tackled Tular and then chased them. It snarled as it buried the bottom part of its face, with its lower, eating mouth, into the carcass and tore pieces off savagely. "What do I have here?" it barked at Zachary, using its other mouth to speak while it continued eating.

Zachary didn't think this was a real question and was too petrified to speak in any case. Worse still, the putrid stench of the Grull's breath was making him sick. He forced himself to calm down and concentrate. There would be no escaping this monster.

But even as he thought this an idea began forming in his mind. The Krug elder had said the portal came back every five minutes. If they could just keep the Grull in this exact spot long enough, the portal would reappear underneath them. If the Grull, like the fungus on the world before, was unable to make the trip through with them, they would be free.

"*Answer me!*" thundered the Grull. "Are you two some kind of mutant Krug?"

"No," said Zachary finally, getting his fear under control. Both he and Jenna were now breathing exclusively through their mouths, trying not to suffocate from the stench that surrounded the towering beast like a toxic cloud. "We aren't from this world. We're softbody people."

"Never heard of such a thing," said the Grull with its speaking mouth, while at the same time using its eating mouth to rip another large piece of flesh from its kill. It turned its attention to Jenna. "You're even punier than this one," it said. "You two are the most pathetic creatures I have ever seen. Slow *and* weak. You're more helpless than a newborn baby Krug."

"*Exactly*," agreed Zachary. "We're certainly not worth *your* time. We couldn't give you any sport at all."

The Grull laughed and spittle and bits of food flew from its mouth. "You're new here or a Krug would have told you that the only sport I enjoy is inflicting terror and suffering on others. I've never tortured a softbody *person* before. I'm looking forward to it."

The spiked monstrosity paused in thought, continuing to hold the two humans in midair as though it could easily do so forever. Although it was totally alien, there was something about its cruel expression that made it clear to the siblings that it was imagining creative ways to inflict as much pain on them as it could, for as long as it could.

"Wait a minute," said the Grull suddenly, its eyes widening. "What am I thinking? I've never *tasted* a softbody person before either."

Zachary shrank back, knowing this was no idle threat. The Grull was the ultimate predator, and it was clearly intrigued with the idea of expanding its culinary horizons.

"I wonder how much of you I can eat and still keep you alive," said the Grull. "I guess there's only one way to find out," it finished icily.

The blood drained from Zachary's face. Of all the ways to die, being eaten alive was one of the most horrific. He shot a panicked look at his sister, and was astonished to find that her eyes were blazing purposefully. "Go for it," she said defiantly to the Grull. "Take a bite. And then see how long you *live* afterwards."

"What's that supposed to mean?"

"What do you think? It means we're the most poisonous species there is."

Zachary's eyes widened. Jenna had come up with a great strategy that just might work.

"Do you think I'm stupid!" roared the Grull.

"Well," said Jenna, "I don't think you're as stupid as you are ugly and smelly."

The Grull blinked rapidly in confusion. "That's better," it said finally, proving its own stupidity. "Poison. Hah. You really expect me to fall for that?"

"Tell me this," said Zachary. "Since we're so slow and weak and helpless, how have we possibly survived here?"

The Grull looked completely blank.

"Because every creature knows we're poisonous and leaves us alone."

The Grull thought about this for a few seconds. "You could be right," it allowed with a deep frown. "Too bad. I guess I'll just have to be satisfied with torturing you to death."

Zachary had been keeping mental track of the time. He guessed that the portal was due to reappear directly under them at any moment. If they could stall just a little longer they were home free.

The Grull took a few steps forward . . . and just as he did so the portal appeared, right on schedule, exactly where he had just been.

Noooo, thought Zachary miserably. They had been so close.

The Grull continued walking, still holding them like dolls in front of its face. It was leaving the portal behind.

"No!" screamed Zachary. "Stop!"

The Grull laughed and continued walking. "Save your pathetic pleas for mercy, they won't do you any good."

Zachary began to panic as they continued to move farther from the portal.

He had to think of something! *And fast.*

But *what*? The Grull was pure cruelty, pure evil, and they couldn't possibly escape its iron grasp. And they had nothing to bargain with. The only way they were going through the portal was if the Grull put them there itself.

Yeah, like that's going to happen, thought Zachary in frustration and despair.

Wait a minute! He thought excitedly. *Maybe that isn't such a crazy idea after all.*

Zachary screamed. He screamed louder and longer than he ever had in his life. He recoiled backwards against the Grull's hand as if he had seen the most terrifying thing in the universe.

The Grull stopped, wondering what was going on.

Zachary turned pale and cowered. He began to whimper as if nearly insane with fear, looking and pointing over the Grull's shoulder.

As the Grull turned to look, Zachary shot a quick look at his sister. *Play along*, he mouthed.

To her credit, Jenna did so without stopping first to wonder why. She began screaming uncontrollably and pointing past the Grull, acting as insanely horrified as her brother.

The Grull studied the forest behind it in confusion. It was empty of animals, since every last creature had long since fled from the vicinity of the world's top predator. So what were they pointing at that scared them so much? And what could possibly scare anyone more than being the prisoner of a Grull, anyway? The Grull was considering these questions when it saw a strange-looking shimmering circle on the ground.

"What is *that?*" it demanded.

Zachary continued his whimpering. "N-n-n-nothing," he stuttered.

The Grull scratched its head with its free claw, with the only one of its four arms not carrying a human or a carcass. "You're terrified—of that?" it said in disbelief.

"No. N-not at all," said Zachary, cringing in fear. "Come on. Weren't you going somewhere to torture us? W-w-what are we waiting for?"

"You're lying to me. You *are* terrified of that thing."

"No we're not," insisted Jenna weakly as she shuddered uncontrollably, displaying acting skills of her own.

"Okay," spat the Grull. "You're not. Then I guess in that case you won't mind if I drop you in that thing?"

"*No!*" screamed Zachary in horror. "*Please!* Do whatever you want. Torture us. *Eat* us. We lied about being poisonous. But you can't be *completely* evil. If you have any mercy at all, don't drop us in that thing."

The Grull was intrigued. "What would happen if I did?"

Zachary's face turned pure white. "It . . . it . . . it . . . h-holds you," he stuttered. "For five or ten minutes. I don't know what it does but it's the most agonizing thing in the universe. I was in it only once. I lost my voice from screaming and I f-f-finally passed out from the pain."

"Really," said the Grull in delight. "That sounds like fun."

"*No!* You can't be *that* cruel."

The Grull laughed. "You really don't know anything about the Grull, do you?"

The towering, armored monster walked to the edge of the portal and extended his human captives over its center. They both closed their eyes and screamed insanely for all they were worth.

Come on, come on, come on, thought Zachary with all of his might as he continued screaming. *Come on! Drop us in. DO IT!*

The Grull took extreme pleasure in their screams and struggles. "Enjoy yourselves," it said happily. "And if you can't, maybe it will make you feel better to know that when you've passed out from the pain, I'll be here to greet you when you wake up."

Wearing a cruel expression on its face and with a maniacal gleam in its eye, the Grull dropped them in the center of the portal.

They felt a minor disorientation and then, once again, they were on firm ground. A world away from the Grull.

They had done it again. They had found a way to snatch victory from the jaws of defeat. If only they could have seen the stupefied look on the Grull's hideous face as they vanished from its world.

Elated, they opened their eyes to see what world they would find themselves on this time.

And what they saw made them almost wish they were back with the Grull.

CHAPTER FOURTEEN

Trespass

Jenna saw it first and shrieked again. Zachary opened his mouth to scream but was so paralyzed by fear that no sound would come out.

It was a giant wasp.

It was about the length of a long car, and it stood on six thin legs watching them through huge compound eyes that bulged out from its face like two black mesh domes. Its red, sweptback body tapered in at the middle and then flared out again toward the back. Its thin wings were pitch black, matching its eyes and the two antennae protruding from its head. Its sleek body made it clear to all observers that this was a creature built for only one purpose: killing.

And it was twenty feet away.

Jenna's knees became weak and she barely managed to remain standing. In escaping the Grull they had jumped from the frying pan into the fire.

The wasp's head darted around and surveyed the area behind itself. "What?" it said in obvious alarm. "What's back there?"

The wasp could talk? Apparently so. In fact, its voice, at least as it was interpreted by the language transformer, was soft and feminine.

It continued to look behind it and backtracked a few steps toward the dumbstruck humans. "I don't see anything. What is it that you're so afraid of?" it asked in confusion.

Zachary tried to speak, but nothing came out. He finally found his voice, but it was thin and high pitched. "You can talk?"

The wasp pivoted its head to face Zachary. "Of course I can talk. Is the danger gone?" it asked worriedly.

"Uhhh . . . yeah," answered Zachary thinly. "False alarm."

The wasp turned its head one last time, just to be sure. It turned back again to face the two humans. "Well that's a relief," it said. "Can you two tell me where I am?"

Jenna exchanged a puzzled look with her brother. "You don't know?" she squeaked, regaining her voice also.

The wasp frowned. "I wouldn't ask you if I knew," it pointed out. "As you can probably tell from my appearance, I'm not from here. I know it's hard to believe, but I think I might be from an entirely different *world* even."

"It's easier to believe than you'd think," said Zachary. "We're not from this world either."

"How remarkable," said the wasp.

"How did *you* get here?" asked Zachary.

"It was the strangest thing. I was with my husband and seven children in my home when the air started shimmering strangely. The next thing I knew I was standing here. About one minute later you two appeared from nowhere and started screaming." The wasp paused. "Frankly, my nerves are shot," she continued, her voice breaking as though she was about to cry. "And I'm so worried about my babies. I hope they're okay." She visibly struggled to bring her emotions under control. "How did you two get here?"

"Our parents disappeared the same way you did," answered Zachary. "And we're looking for them."

"Oh that's terrible. You two are children. You poor things," she said sweetly. "And here I was feeling sorry for myself."

"You didn't know we were kids?" said Jenna.

"Heavens no. I've never seen your kind before, or anything even close."

The wasp began to walk forward to continue the conversation.

Despite knowing that she was intelligent and seemed kind and gentle, the two humans couldn't help but back away nervously at the same pace at which the wasp advanced.

"Are you okay?" she asked gently.

"We're okay," replied Zachary thinly. "But I'm going to be honest with you. You may have never seen anything that looks like us before, but where we're from, we have creatures that look like you."

"Yeah," chimed in Jenna. "Only they're not intelligent, and they're thousands of times smaller."

"Really?" said the wasp with genuine interest.

Jenna nodded. "Really. We call them *wasps*. And the thing is . . . well, the thing is that even though they're tiny compared to us, most humans are terrified of them."

Jenna could handle spiders, for the most part, but once the Lane family had returned home to find a wasp flying around the family room and she had set speed records fleeing the house while her dad tried to kill it. Even her dad, who was usually very brave about spiders and snakes and things, had looked extremely nervous when he had trapped himself inside the house with the wasp holding nothing but a rolled-up magazine for a weapon.

"Terrified?" said the wasp in disbelief. "Why? What are wasps like on your world?"

Zachary shuddered. He knew more about wasps than he wanted to. A few months earlier he had been watching a movie in which alien creatures incubated their young inside living humans. After growing, the alien offspring would exit their human hosts by *bursting through their chests*. His dad had told him these aliens were patterned after wasps. Zachary couldn't believe that anything this grisly was actually happening on Earth, so he researched it further on the Internet. Unbelievably, his dad had been right. There were wasp species that paralyzed insects and then injected them with eggs. Once hatched, the baby wasps, called larva, would devour the still-living insect— *from the inside*. Then they would cut a hole in their dead host and fly out. Just the thought of this made Zachary's skin crawl.

"What are wasps like on Earth?" he repeated, deciding to keep his answer short and skip the gruesome behavior that had just come to mind. "Well," he said simply, "they're very aggressive. And they can fly. But the scary part is that they have stingers with poison in them— and they're not afraid to use them."

The wasp nodded. "I see. Now I understand why you'd be uncomfortable around me. But I can assure you I would never hurt anyone. Many millions of years ago we were similar to the creatures you describe, but our stingers no longer contain any venom nor would we ever use them. And even though we have wings, our kind have grown far too big to fly. We've become a very peaceful species. Please, children, don't be afraid of me," she pleaded. "I'm scared myself. I just want to get back to my family."

They both knew that this being was intelligent and friendly. But the sight of her continued to make them want to run for their lives, regardless of what their brains tried to tell them.

"We know you won't hurt us," said Jenna for them both. "And we're trying to fight it. But I'm afraid this instinctive fear at the sight of you is pretty strong."

The wasp sighed. "I'm so sorry. We have creatures on our world that we are instinctively afraid of, so I understand. I'll leave now so you can avoid any further discomfort. I hope you find your parents," she finished sincerely. She began walking away sadly.

Even when the wasp was moving away from them its movement sent shivers down their spines. Human instincts developed over many thousands of years screamed at them to let the wasp leave. But as she got farther and farther away, their rationality and sense of fairness became stronger than their fear. They had a hurried discussion and quickly reached a decision.

"Don't go," they said in unison. They would just have to suffer until they could get their nerves under control. This poor being seemed like a wonderful . . . person. It wasn't her fault that she looked like a colossal wasp. And it wasn't her problem.

It was *their* problem. And they would have to find a way to overcome it.

The wasp turned to face them.

"We're all in the same boat," explained Zachary. "I think we should explore this world together."

The wasp smiled. "Oh, I couldn't agree more," she said happily. "But are you sure you can overcome your discomfort?"

"Positive," said Zachary with far more certainty than he felt.

"Great," she said, walking up to them.

They forced themselves not to retreat, but it took all the willpower they had.

"My name is Lisgar. I'm a Swishmer."

Jenna and Zachary introduced themselves and the trio began exploring their surroundings.

The world they were on was overcast and misty, and it was obvious that it got plenty of rain on a regular basis. Water was everywhere. Not an ocean, or even a large river, but lakes, ponds, streams, and brooks.

There was no obvious direction to take, so the group chose one at random. The two humans described everything that had happened to them since their parents had disappeared. Throughout the discussion Lisgar was wonderful; always interested and supportive. She always seemed to know the right thing to say and everything about her was gentle and protective—the exact opposite of her fierce and threatening appearance. It wasn't long before they realized her appearance no longer made them uncomfortable.

Lisgar was a member of the only intelligent species on her world. They were vegetarians, and unlike wasps on Earth, their antennae ended in six, finger-like tendrils that were able to hold and grasp objects as easily as could a human hand. Lisgar spoke lovingly about her world and the family that she had left behind, often becoming emotional when she spoke of her children.

They agreed that they would continue their hike until they either ran into a portal or someone who was native to this planet. If they were lucky they would find someone who knew how the portals worked and what had happened to them.

They had been hiking for two hours when they came upon a crop of some kind, planted thickly in regularly spaced rows. A sign of civilization. Perhaps soon they would find someone with some answers.

The plants were bright red and waxy looking. The stalks were taller than corn and twice as thick, and they were grown so closely together they created a red wall that was impossible to see beyond. They walked beside the edge of the crop looking for a native or a farmhouse or any other sign of habitation.

"Did you see that?" said Zachary.

"See what?" asked Lisgar.

"There! There it is again," said Zachary as they continued walking. "The air is shimmering. It's getting more intense as we go forward." Zachary pointed a short distance ahead. "And *there's* its source," he said triumphantly. "A portal."

The trio heard a faint rustle in the crop beside them. Just as they were turning to look there was a break in the crop line and a dozen men—using the term loosely—rushed out and surrounded them with astonishing speed.

Each wore armor and each brandished a sword threateningly. Their feet and legs were enormous and kangaroo-like, although they used them to walk rather than to hop as a kangaroo would. While their faces appeared normal by human standards, each was totally bald and they had one additional outstanding characteristic: they didn't have necks. Their heads swiveled on their shoulders like giant owls.

One of the men pointed nervously to Lisgar. "What about this one?" he said worriedly to another man, one who had a much more ornate sword and different armor than the others and who was obviously their leader.

The leader laughed. "Don't worry about it," he said calmly. "It's just a Swishmer. I haven't seen one of these in years, but they're totally harmless. They may look fearsome but they're as harmless as a puppy and are easily frightened."

The men closed in and shoved the three travelers forward, away from the portal. "Be gentle with them," pleaded Lisgar, despite her obvious fear. "They are not yet adults."

"We know that," snapped the leader. "But it makes no difference. All three of you have trespassed on our world. You are being brought to trial."

"To trial?" said Zachary in disbelief. "But we didn't *know* we were trespassing."

"It doesn't matter," insisted the leader. "Not knowing the law is no excuse. But you can take that up with the

Chief Justice. Just between us, the trial is only a formality anyway. It always ends the same way."

"How?" asked Jenna.

"You will be found guilty," said the leader grimly. "And you will all be executed for your crime."

CHAPTER FIFTEEN

A Last Meal

Jenna gulped. They were in trouble again.

Zachary screamed hysterically and pointed behind their captors.

The men stopped. "What's with him?" one of them asked.

"I don't know," replied the leader. "It looks as though he's terrified of something in that direction." He walked a few paces and swiveled his head from side to side. "Nothing dangerous that I can see. The only thing I see is a portal."

Zachary whimpered. "Please. Execute me. But keep me away from that h-h-horrible thing."

"Don't worry. I don't plan on letting you *near* a portal," said the leader. He rubbed his bald head in puzzlement. "Although, if it were *me* facing an execution, I would desperately *want* to get to a portal so I could escape. Very strange."

Zachary's whimpering and cowering stopped abruptly. He looked at Jenna and shrugged his shoulders. "Oh well," he said. "Worth a try."

Jenna couldn't help but smile.

"So you know all about portals and transporting between worlds, huh?" said Zachary to the leader.

"Of course we do. We have thousands of these things leading to our world, and thousands more leading off. That's why we've set a strict no-trespassing policy."

"So how do the portals work?" asked Zachary casually, trying to hide his eagerness.

The leader smiled. "Good try. We have many laws here. One of them is that we can't share information about portals with someone from another world."

Figures, thought Zachary in frustration.

The rest of the trip was made in silence. After walking for two hours the group came to a giant stone wall, three stories tall and extending in both directions for as far as the eye could see. Sentries were posted at even intervals along its top.

They were led through a gate and into the city. The buildings inside were all made of stone, but the builders had used different types and colors to create intricate and unusual patterns. The buildings themselves formed geometric shapes of great variety and complexity. They were led inside a blue, egg-shaped building and marched down wide stone stairs to a dark, damp, and musky basement.

They finally stopped before a small stone cell with a row of bars forming the outer wall. The leader opened the bars, shoved the two humans and Lisgar inside, and locked the bars behind them. "You'll all be staying here until your trial tomorrow morning," he announced as his men began leaving.

When the last of their captors left, the trio talked at length about the trial and what they might be facing, but finally decided to change the subject. The more they talked about it, the more worried they became, and they knew that further discussion wouldn't help them.

Soon after they arrived in the prison cell, Lisgar was forcibly removed to undergo an interrogation, and Zachary and Jenna got the sense that the people of this planet really didn't like or trust insect species. The kids had grown so fond of her that her absence further worsened their already bleak moods.

Both kids slumped down against the steel bars. "You think we're ever gonna see Mom and Dad again," said Jenna softly, and Zachary could tell she was seconds away from bursting into tears once again.

It was hard to blame her. His eyes were moist as well, and if she broke down, he wouldn't be far behind.

What if their parents were dead already? And even if they were still alive, as Wyland had claimed, it seemed impossible to believe he and Jenna could find them. He and his sister were incredibly lucky to still be alive, themselves, and he wondered just how much longer they could survive. If all worlds were like those they had been on so far, it would be a miracle for them to last a week.

But they had to find some way to stay strong and positive. Even with the most positive attitude in the world, they had very little chance of succeeding. But if they gave into despair, they had no chance at all.

Zachary knew it was important that they not dwell on just how hopeless things were. They needed to keep trying to find the humor in things, whenever possible, and convince themselves they would find their parents and make it back home alive. They couldn't let grisly images of their parents, lying dead on an unknown world, creep into their imaginations, and they couldn't let their longing for home weaken their will.

The moisture began to pool in Jenna's eyes, and Zachary knew he had to find a way to distract her from their desperate situation. Last time his attempt to do this had been clumsy and a total failure, and he couldn't afford for this to happen again.

"Boy, I have to tell you," he began. "I'm feeling more confident than ever about things. This is all going to work out. I'm *sure* of it."

Jenna shook her head as if she hadn't heard right. He had no doubt that the surprise of his statement had pulled her mind away from negative thoughts, at least for the moment.

"How can you possibly say that?" she said.

"Easily," he replied cheerfully. "You just have to move your mouth." He grabbed his jaw with his right hand and moved it up and down. "This . . . is . . . all . . . going . . . to . . . work . . . out," he said slowly as he moved his jaw. "See. That wasn't hard at all."

Jenna couldn't help but smile. They were in the middle of a dungeon on a hopeless quest, and Zachary was clowning around. And it was working. Her mood was improving. "You really think we have a chance?"

"Absolutely!" said Zachary, doing a good job of faking enthusiasm. "You've been even more impressive than I thought you'd be."

Jenna rolled her eyes. "Yeah, real impressive. Are you forgetting about the ping-pong ball?"

"Not at all. That was just bad luck. And you *weren't* clumsy. I just said that because I didn't want to admit I was the one who screwed up. I didn't pull the car close enough. I thought you might have trouble grabbing it. But I was in my usual hurry and didn't move closer."

Jenna brightened. "Really?" she said.

"Really," lied Zachary.

Jenna smiled. "All right then," she said. "Let's get out of this prison and get on with finding Mom and Dad."

"Piece of cake," said Zachary, returning her smile.

But this time, his smile was real. Focusing on the needs of someone other than himself was something he had rarely done before. But knowing he had lifted his sister's spirits rather than drowned them had lifted his own spirits in ways he wouldn't have guessed. Who knew? Was this why people spent so much time helping others?

Now that he had successfully improved Jenna's mood, Zachary told her funny stories about his classmates to pass the time and keep their minds off their situation until Lisgar was returned to their cell, thirty minutes later.

As soon as she was locked inside the guard turned toward the two humans. "Are you hungry?" he asked. "You have the right to a last meal."

Zachary and Jenna realized they were starving. They told him so. Neither had eaten anything but a few forkfuls of their mother's horrible chicken dish when this all began—it seemed like an eternity ago.

"I'm starving too," added Lisgar.

Five minutes later the two humans were each handed a portion of food, dumped in the center of a flat metal plate. It was a mush that was probably made from the crop they had seen growing outside. They tasted it cautiously. It was a little bland, but their hunger wouldn't allow them to be picky. Unfortunately, there wasn't very much of it.

The man who had given them the food began walking away. "Wait a second," Jenna called out to him. "What about Lisgar? Where's her food?"

"She doesn't get any," replied the man.

"Why not?" demanded Zachary.

"I don't know. That's just the rule. You're from a human-type world so you get a meal. The thing with you is from an insect-type world so she doesn't." The man walked off, clearly not intending to argue about it.

"That's horrible," complained Jenna. "It's so unfair."

"It's okay, Sweetheart," said Lisgar motherly. "Sometimes things aren't fair."

"You can have some of ours," offered Jenna. Zachary nodded his agreement.

"That's very sweet of you. But I'll be fine."

"We insist," said Zachary. "You're just as hungry as we are. And we're a team."

"But you two are still growing and—"

"We won't take no for an answer," interrupted Jenna.

Lisgar smiled gently. "Well if you're going to be that insistent," she said, obviously touched by their gesture, "then I will have a tiny bit. Thank you both."

"You're very welcome," said Jenna. "It wouldn't be a meal without you."

Zachary frowned. "Now we just have to find a way to make sure this isn't the last meal we ever have."

CHAPTER SIXTEEN

The Challenge

After hours of conversation, during which Jenna and Zachary grew ever fonder of their gentle wasp companion, followed by a fitful night's sleep, the three prisoners were led from their cell into a small octagonal building. The walls were made of smooth, yellow stone, and brightly colored jewels were imbedded in the floor and ceiling in triangular patterns.

The prisoners were marched in front of a man they were told was the Chief Justice of the world. A world named Mesrobia. Five guards, heavily armed, stood behind the prisoners.

The Chief Justice was behind an elegant, green-marble table, seated on a magnificent golden chair, wide enough to hold his massive kangaroo legs. His face showed more age than the others of his kind they had seen, and he carried himself with an air of authority. He looked down at the docket in front of him. "What do we have today," he muttered to himself. "Let's see. Two humans, brother and sister. And a Swishmer. Interesting mix."

He looked up and cleared his throat. "The three of you have been accused of trespassing on our world," he announced, his voice now booming and taking on an official tone. "How do you plead?"

"Not guilty," they all said at once.

"*Of course you're guilty!*" snapped the Chief Justice impatiently. "You're here, aren't you? On Mesrobia. On our world."

"We know that, Your . . . ahh . . . Your Justice-ship," stammered Zachary.

"No need for titles. We don't stand on formality here."

Zachary nodded. "You see, the thing is," he continued, "none of us are here on purpose, and we knew nothing about your trespassing law."

"Makes no difference," snapped the Chief Justice. "Ignorance of the law is no excuse. You'll notice I didn't accuse you of *knowingly* trespassing—just trespassing."

"But we don't understand," said Lisgar. "We haven't hurt anyone or anything. And we'd be happy to leave your world immediately. Why such a stiff and inflexible penalty?"

"I assure you it is quite necessary. At one time we Mesrobians had no such law and it was mayhem here. Our world has thousands of portals and we had an inordinate amount of traffic coming through from every world you can imagine. It was a terrible problem.

Criminals came to Mesrobia to escape their own justice system. And many of the species couldn't get along for one reason or another. Fighting broke out almost every day. There were so many different species from different worlds it was impossible to keep them all straight. Mesrobia was overcome by violence, confusion, chaos, and disorder. Something had to be done."

The Chief Justice paused. "So twenty years ago, I made our world strictly off-limits to outsiders. Visitors were allowed to come here by invitation only. Anyone who knowingly trespassed would be executed."

"That makes sense," said Zachary. "Especially the *knowingly* part."

The Chief Justice shook his head, or swiveled it back and forth at any rate. "It didn't work. We had just as much traffic as before. Whenever we tried to enforce our law the criminals would insist that they were here by accident, or didn't know the law, and we would have to let them go. Finally, we changed the law so that any trespassing was punishable by execution. *Any* trespassing. Regardless of the circumstances. And I'm happy to report that we've had very little problem since."

"But now that you have this law and the other worlds know it, no one would be crazy enough to come here on purpose," insisted Zachary. "The only beings who come here now are the ones who really do stumble on your world by accident. The ones who really are innocent."

"Could be true," agreed the Chief Justice. "Probably is. That's an unfortunate side effect of a very successful law."

"There has to be some way to fix the law so that it doesn't punish the innocent," said Jenna.

"Maybe," grumbled the Chief Justice. "Maybe not. I'll consider it over the next few years and see if I can come up with something," he said, as though the matter were entirely settled. "In the meanwhile, I have reached my decision." He paused for effect. "I find the three prisoners guilty as charged of the crime of trespassing."

He turned to the guards. "Take them out and have them executed."

The guards came forward.

"Wait a minute," ordered the Chief Justice, holding up his hand. "I almost forgot. We have a custom. Before you're executed, I will answer one question from each of you. Whatever it is, if I know the answer I will tell you—as long as it doesn't have to do with the workings of the portals." He looked at Lisgar. "Ask your question," he told her.

"Are my children okay?" she asked worriedly.

"I don't have any idea," said the Chief Justice. He turned to Jenna. "Next question please."

Jenna didn't hesitate. This was her chance to find out about her parents. "Have you seen any more of our kind here during the past six months?"

"No," replied the Chief Justice. "We are aware of every visitor to our world, and you are the first of your kind to ever visit Mesrobia."

Jenna lowered her eyes and sighed. It didn't matter, she thought. They were about to be executed anyway. What had she expected, that this was like in the movies? That she'd learn her parents were nearby and they would rescue her at the last second?

"Your turn," said the Chief Justice to Zachary. "Ask your question."

Zachary paused for a long while, deep in thought. Finally, he stared deep into the Chief Justice's eyes and said, "How can we save ourselves from this execution?"

The Chief Justice laughed. "Bravo," he said, clapping lightly. "You'd be surprised how few prisoners ask that particular question. You never know until you ask, do you? We very much respect cleverness here. Well done."

He leaned forward toward Zachary. "Now that you've asked, it turns out that there is a way; one way only. You have to petition for citizenship. If you become a citizen of our world, then you wouldn't be trespassing. You'd be considered one of us. You could then do as you please: stay on Mesrobia, go back to your original world, or go on to another world of your choice."

Zachary's eyes widened. "You know how to send us back to our original world?" he said.

"Absolutely. But you have to become a citizen first."

"How?"

"It's not easy, I can assure you. You would have to pass the *Challenge*. I told you we respect cleverness here. You and your sister would work as a team. You would have to prove that you're worthy of being Mesrobians. Together you would have to solve six riddles of various levels of difficulty."

Jenna barely managed to stop herself from grinning in relief. Riddles. *Fantastic*. Her brother was the best riddle solver she had ever known.

"That's it?" said Zachary. "Solve six riddles and we're honorary Mesrobians?"

"Solving riddles is a good test of reasoning. We pride ourselves on being a very clever species. And we obviously can't give a physical challenge since different species have quite different physical abilities. But don't think it will be easy. Most Challengers can solve one or two of the riddles, but very few have ever been able to solve all six."

"But every Mesrobian can solve them, right?" said Jenna.

The Chief Justice frowned. "Well, actually . . . no."

"But I thought it was a test to see if we were clever enough to be one of you," said Zachary.

"Well, I imagine that some of us could do it. But we were born on Mesrobia, so we don't have to prove ourselves worthy. If you want to be considered a citizen, you have to prove yourselves to be as worthy as the very best of us."

"Uh-huh," said Zachary, not fully agreeing with this logic but knowing that an argument wouldn't help. Besides, it didn't matter how difficult the Challenge was. It was definitely better than their immediate alternative. "We're prepared to take your Challenge. We petition for citizenship."

The Chief Justice beamed. "Fantastic! We haven't had a Challenge in a long time. They certainly spice things up around here. We can start in about an hour. I'll have to spread the word so we can gather a crowd to watch the festivities. We'll set up chairs in the grand ballroom."

He turned to the guards again. "In the meanwhile, take this other prisoner out and have her executed."

"I petition for citizenship, also," said Lisgar immediately.

The Chief Justice swiveled his head back and forth. "You can't. You're from an insect world. The law is very clear. Only those from human worlds have this option." He turned once more to the guards. "What are you waiting for," he barked. "I want her executed within the hour."

With that the guards prodded Lisgar with their swords and began roughly leading her away.

CHAPTER SEVENTEEN

The Stakes Rise

"Wait!" yelled Jenna. "You can't do that!"

"Of course I can," responded the Chief Justice. "It's the law."

"We can vouch for Lisgar," insisted Jenna. "She's a wonderful person. Who cares that she has a wasp body? She's every bit as worthy as we are to become a citizen."

"It doesn't matter," said the Chief Justice firmly. "The law is the law . . . and it's very clear in this matter. Before the trespassing law was initiated we especially had trouble with the insect worlds, so we made even harsher laws for them."

"Did you ever have trouble with a Swishmer?" asked Zachary.

The Chief Justice considered. "Well, no . . . I don't think so. But it doesn't matter."

"It does to us," said Jenna defiantly.

"No member of an insect world," said the Chief Justice, "can take the Challenge. Period. That is the law." The Chief Justice waved his hands and the guards continued marching Lisgar to the door.

"Wait a second," said Zachary in desperation. "The law says that no member of an insect world can take the Challenge. But can someone else take it for them?"

The Chief Justice grimaced. These humans never seemed to give up. Lisgar had just entered the open doorway. "Hold on again," he instructed the guards.

"I don't know," he said to Zachary. "I have to admit that it has never really come up. No one has ever been insane enough to want to take the Challenge for a member of an insect world."

The Chief Justice's head swiveled back and forth for a few seconds and it was obvious he was deep in thought. "I suppose if a being *wanted* to do this, since we have no law against it, I would allow it," he said finally.

Zachary looked at his sister. She nodded vigorously. "Then we will take it for Lisgar," he said.

The Chief Justice furrowed his brow in disapproval. Finally, he waved his hand for the guards to bring Lisgar back into the room. "Before you make a final decision, you should know this: if you take it for her you must answer an additional three riddles. And it's all or nothing. Either all of you become citizens or none of you do. If you only had to answer six riddles correctly your chances of passing the Challenge are extremely slim—but at least you would have some chance. With nine you are signing not just this Swishmer's death warrant but yours as well. Are you positive you want to do this?"

"Let me be sure I'm getting this right," said Zachary. "If we pass the Challenge, you'll return Lisgar to her world, unharmed, and let us go."

"Correct."

Zachary didn't hesitate. "Then we're positive."

"No!" pleaded Lisgar from the back of the room as the guards brought her forward. "You can't do this for me!"

"Silence!" snapped the Chief Justice. "They have made their decision. I don't want to hear another word out of you."

Zachary stared at the Chief Justice defiantly. "And since you think that passing the Challenge is now impossible," he said, "I propose something else. I propose adding a tenth riddle. If we solve all ten, you agree to change your law so that it doesn't punish innocent, um . . . beings."

"Absolutely not! That's the most ridiculous proposition I've ever heard. Why would I possibly agree to it?"

"Why not? You're positive we can't do it anyway, so what have you got to lose? Besides, you know the law needs to be changed. If you're so clever you should be able to figure out a way to design a successful law that's *fair*." Zachary raised his eyebrows. "And it might also make for a more interesting contest."

The Chief Justice frowned. Then he smiled. Then he laughed. "Agreed," he said finally. "You certainly have guts, I'll say that much for you. Unfortunately for you, the Challenge doesn't measure guts. Let's hope for your sake that you're also good at solving riddles."

A little more than an hour later the three prisoners found themselves in a vast ballroom, with a domed ceiling five stories high. Enormous, diamond-shaped chandeliers, made of multicolored crystal, hung down at even intervals to flood the room with a bright, rose-tinted light. The walls and floor of the ballroom were made of the same green-colored marble they had already seen several times. The room was packed wall to wall with Mesrobians. Word had spread fast and the interest in the contest was enormous.

Finally, everything was set. The riddles had been selected. Lisgar was held, heavily guarded, at the back of the room, horrified that the humans were decreasing their own chance of survival for her. The Chief Justice sat at the front of the room at a small table and the contestants faced him, with their backs to the crowd, behind individual podiums made of smooth, yellow stone.

The Chief Justice held up his hand for silence and the roar from the large crowd gradually died out. "You all know why we are here," he began, his booming voice echoing around the vast room. "The human boy, Zachary Lane, and the human girl, Jenna Lane, have petitioned for Mesrobian citizenship and have agreed to take our Challenge. Furthermore, they will also be taking the Challenge in an effort to win citizenship for the Swishmer, Lisgar."

There was a loud murmur from the crowd. This was an unprecedented development. Why would anyone offer to take the Challenge to save someone from an insect world?

The Chief Justice waited for the murmur to die down. "Finally," he continued, "they will need to do more than answer nine riddles to earn their own and the Swishmer's citizenship. In order to win the Challenge, they have agreed to answer *ten* riddles. In exchange, if they are successful, I have agreed to revise our trespassing laws."

There was a collective gasp of disbelief from the crowd. There had never, ever, been a Challenge like this one. Very few Mesrobians had believed they could answer six riddles successfully, but not a single spectator in the vast crowd believed they could answer ten.

The Chief Justice was delighted by the reaction but pretended not to notice. "The humans will work as a team. But there will be no discussion or communication allowed between them. I will read the riddles out loud and then display them in writing on this easel behind me for the contestants and the spectators to use for reference. Zachary will be given the first one and will have two minutes to answer it correctly. If he is unable to solve it, Jenna will have two minutes to solve it. If the first riddle is solved, the next riddle will be given first to

Jenna to attempt, and then to Zachary if she is unsuccessful. And so on." He looked at the contestants. "Any questions?"

"Let's get this started," said Zachary, trying to sound far more confident than he felt.

It was true that he was very good at solving riddles, but even the best riddle-solver in the world couldn't get every one. And that's exactly what they had to do. If they were stumped by even a single riddle, the Challenge was over.

Zachary braced himself. There was no room for error. He knew that they had to be perfect.

Because their very lives depended on it.

CHAPTER EIGHTEEN

Riddles

"Riddle number one," said the Chief Justice. *From what can you take away the whole—and still have some left?*"

Zachary let out a sigh of relief. This one was relatively easy as riddles went and he came to the answer almost immediately. If they all stayed this easy they were in good shape. "The word *Wholesome*," he answered. "Take away WHOLE and you still have SOME left."

"Ohhh," murmured the crowd appreciatively.

"Correct," said the Chief Justice. He cleared his throat. "Riddle number two. *Yesterday I threw a ball. It went ten feet, stopped, reversed direction, and then returned to me. It didn't hit anything and I didn't have a string attached. How did I do it?*"

Jenna took a deep breath and tried to steady her nerves. She had never been as good as Zachary was at riddles but she wasn't bad either. And she had never thought so clearly. She reached in her pocket and felt the reassuring presence of the small generator. Relax, she told herself, and let the thoughts flow freely.

Yesss. There it was. The answer. "You threw the ball ten feet straight up into the air. When it reached its highest point, it stopped, reversed direction, and fell back down to you."

There was another murmur of appreciation from the crowd. "Correct," the Chief Justice said again.

He looked at Zachary. "Riddle number three. *Two men are playing checkers. They play three games. Each man wins two of them. How is this possible?*"

Zachary thought a moment and then smiled. Perhaps the Chief Justice was starting with very simple riddles because he knew they had a long way to go and wanted to build the drama. But so far, so good, he thought. "The two men aren't playing each other," he answered.

"Correct," said the Chief Justice yet again.

The reaction from the crowd was growing after every riddle. These were worthy contestants, indeed.

"Riddle number four," the Chief Justice said to Jenna. "*What word is spelled wrong in every dictionary ever printed?*"

Jenna arrived at the answer almost immediately. Her brief stay on Orum, where everything was taken literally, had been great preparation for this contest. "The word *wrong*," she answered firmly.

"Correct again," said the Chief Justice, becoming impressed.

A hush came over the crowd. They were intrigued. No team had ever managed to solve four riddles so quickly.

"Riddle number five:
You can find me in darkness but never in light
I am present in daytime but absent in night
I'm most of your daddy but none of your mom
I'm there for the dance, but never the prom
Who am I?"

Zachary concentrated. He knew right away that this was going to be very tough. What in the world could satisfy all of these conditions? *Most of your daddy but none of your mom*, he read from the easel. What nonsense was this?

He studied the poem again. The thing he was looking for could be found in darkness, daytime, daddy, and dances, and was absent from light, night, moms, and proms. So what did darkness, daytime, daddy and dances have in common? *Darkness, daytime, daddy, and dances*, he mouthed to himself, *darkness, daytime, daddy, and dances*. It was almost a tongue twister, he realized, although not a very good one. *She sells seashells by the seashore*. Bet you can't say that five times fast.

And then the answer hit him right between the eyes and it was hard to believe he had not solved it earlier. His brain must be getting tired. "The answer is that you are the letter D," he said simply. The letter D did not appear in light, night, mom or prom, but was present once each in darkness, dances, and daytime, and three times in the five-letter word *daddy*. Or, to put it another way, *most of your "daddy"* was made up of D's, *but none of your "mom"*.

"Correct," said the Chief Justice once again, and this time the crowd actually applauded.

The Chief Justice paused. They had made it easily through five riddles. Impressive indeed. But that still left five more. The contest was far from over.

"Riddle number six. *What word has KST in its middle, in the beginning, and at the end? Also, the word only has a single K, a single S, and a single T in it.*"

Jenna strained this time. This one was surely impossible. Zachary had once given her some hints on how to solve riddles. He had told her to just focus on one piece at a time. Don't get panicked by trying to solve it all. Many times you could solve the whole puzzle by solving half.

She considered the first part alone. *What word has KST in its middle, in the beginning, and at the end.*

And then it became instantly obvious. Her experiences on Orum had paid off again. If she took the question literally it read: *What word has KST in its middle, IN, the beginning, AND, at the end.*

"Inkstand," she announced happily. The word began with IN, ended with AND, and had KST in the middle. And the answer satisfied the conditions of the second part of the riddle; the letters K, S, and T were each used only once.

The Chief Justice indicated she was right and the crowd applauded vigorously. The contestants had answered six riddles—without *either* of them missing a single one. It was unheard of. If they hadn't foolishly volunteered to make the Challenge more difficult by adding the Swishmer they would have been home free already.

"Quiet down," the Chief Justice instructed the crowd. His head swiveled back toward Zachary to resume. "Riddle number seven. Solve the following poem:

Pronounced as one letter and written with three
Two letters there are, and two only in me
I provide information, I'm brown, blue and gray
I'm read from both ends, and the same either way."

Zachary couldn't help but smile as he reread the riddle from the easel. This should be reasonably easy. The first part of the first line was the key. *Pronounced as one letter*. He was looking for a word that was pronounced the same as a single letter. That narrowed the answer down to one of the letters in the alphabet.

He went through them quickly. BEE? It was *pronounced with one letter and written with three*. And it only had two letters, B and E in it, satisfying the second requirement; *two letters there are and two only in me*.

But Zachary couldn't see how it satisfied the rest of the poem.

How about the letter C? SEA? SEE?

SEA required three letters so it was out. SEE didn't make it past the third line of the poem.

Q and T quickly came to mind. CUE as in cue-ball. A TEE for golf. TEA to drink. No, these didn't work. R? Which would give him OUR and ARE. No, these didn't work either. He had found several words that satisfied the first two lines of the riddle but none could satisfy the third.

What about I? EYE. He considered. It satisfied the first two lines of the riddle. What about the third. *I provide information, I'm brown, blue and gray*. Yes, he thought excitedly, it fit. An eye was used to provide information about what things looked like. And an eye *could* be brown blue or gray in color.

Now for the final test. *I'm read from both ends, and the same either way. It worked*. The word was the same read backwards or forewords; E-Y-E.

Zachary looked up at the Chief Justice. "EYE," he said, and then spelled it.

The Chief Justice nodded. *Amazing*. He had never encountered contestants so good at riddle solving. By now he was fully expecting them to solve every one. "Correct again," he said.

Now it was Jenna's turn once more. "Riddle number eight. *What is bigger than the universe, dead people eat it, and if living people eat it, they die?*"

Jenna's heart sank. This one was trouble. She forced herself not to panic. If she had solved the others, she could solve this one.

But how? It was impossible right off the bat. Bigger than the universe? *Nothing* was bigger than the universe. By definition, it was the biggest thing there was.

The answer hit her like a bolt of lightning. Of course. That was it. *Nothing* was bigger than the universe. The answer was NOTHING. NOTHING was bigger than the universe. Dead people ate NOTHING. If living people ate NOTHING they would soon die.

"Nothing," she said, elated. She wasn't letting herself or Zachary down. At this rate they would win the Challenge for sure.

The crowd broke out in cheers once again. They began chanting, "Humans . . . Humans . . . Humans," over and over again.

The Chief Justice was also astonished by the contestant's accomplishments so far, but this was a formal occasion and he couldn't allow himself the luxury of becoming a fan. He had to keep order. "Enough!" he roared at the crowd. "If I hear another outbreak I'll stop the Challenge."

The Chief Justice turned toward Zachary. "Riddle number nine," he said. "*Find the two words that complete the following statement: MADAM, IN EDEN, blank, blank."*

Zachary panicked. Was that the entire riddle? There had to be more to it.

Thankfully, the Chief Justice continued. "Here is a hint. The following statements can each lead you to the answer:

TEN ANIMALS I SLAM IN A NET
WAS IT A CAR OR A CAT I SAW?
NOW, SIR, A WAR IS WON
CAN I ATTAIN A 'C'
A MAN, A PLAN, A CANAL, PANAMA."

What in the world? thought Zachary, deeply worried for the first time. The clues didn't seem to have anything to do with the statement he had to finish. He scratched his head and focused all of his concentration on finding some hidden connection.

As he struggled to find the answer a bead of sweat formed on his forehead and slowly rolled down his face. He thought his brain would explode he was thinking so hard. But he was stumped.

"Your time is up," announced the Chief Justice, sounding disappointed. They were not infallible after all.

The spectators all gasped in unison. The boy had missed one. He had tripped and fallen just a single step from the finish line.

"Jenna," continued the Chief Justice. "You now have two minutes to come up with the correct answer. If you don't the contest is over."

Jenna gulped. The contest was as good as over, then. They were as good as dead. She had studied the puzzle the entire time Zachary was working on it and had come up with nothing. Two additional minutes wouldn't help any. Her brother was the king of riddles. If *he* couldn't solve it there was no way in the world that *she* could.

She glanced over at Zachary hopelessly. She had expected his expression to be vacant. She expected a look of defeat. A look that said, *it's all over now, my moronic sister will never solve it.* But instead, his eyes met hers and he made a determined fist and shook it in front of him. He nodded his head slightly as if to say, *go ahead, Jen, show them how it's done.*

Maybe she could. Zachary certainly had faith in her. And she did feel remarkably sharp. She reached in her pocket and clutched the generator nervously. It was time for her to step up to the plate. It was now or never.

She hastily reread the clues from the easel on which the Chief Justice had placed the riddle in writing. The meaning of the phrases wasn't helpful. She had determined that herself. And Zachary's failure had only made her more certain.

Wait a minute, she thought. The Chief Justice had said that the statements could *each* lead them to the answer.

Not all the statements, *taken together*. But each one by themselves. Any one of them alone would do it.

But how? It wasn't their meaning. It must be something about *how* they were written. Just like in the riddle Zachary had solved. The answer had been EYE. The fact that you could read it the same way backwards and forwards had nothing to do with the meaning of the word. It related to *how* it was written.

Wait a second. It *couldn't* be that easy. She looked at the first line and almost screamed from excitement. *It was*.

TEN ANIMALS I SLAM IN A NET

If she started from the end and read backwards, and didn't worry about spaces between words—it said the same thing as it did starting from the beginning.

She quickly tried reading the others backwards.

WAS IT A CAR OR A CAT I SAW?
NOW, SIR, A WAR IS WON
CAN I ATTAIN A "C"
A MAN, A PLAN, A CANAL, PANAMA

It was true for all of them. Each demonstrated how to solve the riddle; *MADAM IN EDEN, blank, blank*. She studied the phrase she had to complete, searching for the word EDEN going backwards. There it was. Madam i**N EDE**n. What followed EDEN in the backwards direction? IMADAM. *I'm Adam*. The whole statement was, MADAM, IN EDEN, I'M ADAM.

"Your time is . . ."

"I'm Adam!" shouted Jenna just under the wire, interrupting the Chief Justice.

A hush fell over the crowd. They looked at the Chief Justice in fascination. Was this the right answer? Most of them had no idea.

The Chief Justice smiled, surprised by how relieved he felt. These humans had grown on him even more than he had thought. His eyes sparkled. "Correct," he announced enthusiastically, unable to completely hide his emotions.

Zachary caught his sister's eye and shot her an exhilarated look that said, *way to go, Jen.*

Jenna grinned broadly. She had done it! She had saved the team. Now they simply had to answer a single riddle and they were home free.

The crowd was stunned into silence. The girl's answer had been right. The tension had been nearly unbearable and the human girl had solved the riddle with less than a second to go. Talk about drama. They had already seen history made several riddles before. But these humans were now on the verge of the impossible.

The Chief Justice paused for an unusually long period of time to collect himself and build the suspense. "Riddle number ten," he said to Jenna. "The final riddle." Not a sound could be heard in the massive room, not even breathing. The spectators were on the edge of their seats. "Make the equation, $5 + 5 + 5 = 550$ true by adding a single line."

Jenna was still glowing from her triumph over the last riddle. Her confidence was at an all time high. If they solved this they would win. They would not be executed. Lisgar would be returned to her home and her children. Even Mesrobia's unfair law would be changed.

She strained. What was the trick? She looked at the numbers from every angle she could think of, adding a 1 to different parts of the equation, but came up empty. She began to panic. This should be so easy. Especially compared to some of the other riddles they had solved. But it just wouldn't come to her.

"Your time is up," announced the Chief Justice in a stunned voice. "Zachary, you have two minutes."

Jenna expected that her brother had already solved it during her two minutes and would immediately shout out the answer. But he did not. In fact he looked perplexed as he fought to come up with the answer. This should be an easy one, he told himself. But he was mentally exhausted and it somehow seemed impossible. What could the answer be? He couldn't fail now after they had come so far. Their lives depended on it.

"Your . . . time . . . is . . . up," said the Chief Justice slowly, trying to give Zachary an extra moment to shout an answer just under the wire as his sister had done. But this time, no answer was given. This time, no last second heroics would save them from defeat.

There were gasps of dismay from the spectators. They had lost.

"The correct answer is that you add a slanted line to the first plus sign, turning it into a four. The equation would then read 5 4 5 + 5 = 550."

Zachary and Jenna looked at each other in disbelief. It had been so simple. Like the answer to all riddles it seemed ridiculously obvious once it was given. They had been so close to victory that they could taste it. It would have been better to have missed the first one rather than fail just when total victory was finally within their grasp. They were devastated.

The Chief Justice was stunned. They had answered riddles more difficult than this one. The humans would have won their lives and that of the Swishmer if only the boy hadn't been so determined to fix the trespassing law. But they had ultimately failed. They had gone further than any contestants in history only to end up losing the Challenge in the end.

"Zachary and Jenna Lane, you have been found unworthy of becoming citizens of our world," decreed the Chief Justice, knowing that no alien beings had ever been *more* worthy. "Your original sentence for the crime of trespassing stands, as does Lisgar's."

He frowned, clearly unhappy with the outcome. They had made him a believer and after answering nine riddles he knew they were deserving of citizenship. But it wasn't his idea to add a tenth riddle—it was theirs. He had announced the rules of the Challenge at the very beginning. As much as he wished he had a way out, his hands were tied.

"But because of your excellent performance," he continued. "I would like to bestow a high honor upon you."

They brightened. That sounded good. Perhaps the Chief Justice had the power to give them a less . . . final . . . sentence.

The Chief Justice leaned forward. "I will give you the honor of choosing the method of your execution.

CHAPTER NINTEEN

A Method of Execution

"Bring the Swishmer forward," commanded the Chief Justice. "She will stand with the humans."

The guards prodded Lisgar to the front of the room. Her bulging compound eyes were moist with emotion. Eyes Jenna and Zachary had once thought were hideous had miraculously become warm and expressive as they had gotten to know her.

"You were wonderful," she whispered softly as she approached them. "This is all my fault." She lowered her head sadly and tried to gather her emotions. "If you hadn't tried to help me, you'd be free. I'm so sorry."

"It wasn't your fault," insisted Jenna. "You've become our friend. We couldn't just let them execute you."

"You two are very special," said Lisgar warmly, now directly beside them.

The Chief Justice cleared his throat loudly to get the full attention of the three visitors standing before him.

"We have two forms of execution here in Mesrobia," he announced. "We can feed you to a Smorg or we can throw you over a cliff."

Both kids gulped. Neither knew what a Smorg was but they sure didn't want to find out.

He directed his attention at the two humans. "As is our custom, the next statement one of you makes will decide your fate. If it is *true* we will feed you to a Smorg. If it is *false* we will throw you over a cliff." He folded his arms. "We await your statement."

Jenna felt sick to her stomach. She glanced at her brother and could tell his mind was racing. What was he thinking about at this point? Was there some way to make a statement that wouldn't result in a choice?

There was.

What if the Chief Justice didn't know if a statement was true or false? They could say, "There are exactly a billion grains of sand in all the beaches of Mesrobia." The only way the Mesrobians would ever know if the statement was true or false would be to count.

"Oh, and one more thing," said the Chief Justice, as if reading her mind. "I have to be able to easily determine if your statement is true or false."

Zachary groaned. He must have had the same idea she had, thought Jenna. That was it, then. They were finished.

She looked over to her brother and could tell that he was continuing to think furiously, redoubling his efforts.

She waited, holding her breath, hoping he would pull off a miracle and find some clever way to change their fate.

Wait a minute, she thought. What was she doing? They were moments away from being executed and she was leaving their fate entirely up to her brother. Hadn't she shown that she could think also? At least with the help of her parents' generator. Hadn't she, not moments before, even answered a riddle that had stumped her brother. She shouldn't just rely entirely on Zachary.

She put her mind back to the problem.

The Chief Justice was waiting for one of them to make a statement. What if she didn't make an absolute statement? What if she put a word in the statement like *might*, or *could? It might rain tomorrow.*

No, that didn't work. That was true. Even if the forecast didn't call for rain, it *might* rain anyway. She continued thinking furiously.

The Chief Justice looked at Zachary. "You have had plenty of time to decide your fate. Make your statement, *now*, or I will decide the method of execution for you."

Zachary was horrified. He had been unable to think of anything to save them. This was really it then. He had finally run into a situation he couldn't talk, bluff, or trick his way out of. Well, he wouldn't go quietly, he resolved. Once he was outside the guards just might find him to be more slippery than they imagined.

Zachary opened his mouth to speak . . . and heard his sister's voice from beside him. "Lisgar, Zachary, and

I will be thrown over a cliff," she said robotically. Her eyes were closed and her face scrunched up in total concentration.

Zachary stared at his sister in confusion. Now that she had pulled this statement out of some deeply focused recess of her brain her face relaxed. She glanced at him and did something he wouldn't have expected in a million years. *She winked*. Very quickly, but unmistakably. What in the world did she have in mind?

"A strange statement," observed the Chief Justice. "But one that will suffice for our purposes." He cleared his throat and using his loudest, most formal voice said, "For the record, the human girl, Jenna Lane, has made a statement on behalf of the condemned prisoners in accordance with our customs. Her official statement is, 'Lisgar, Zachary, and I will be thrown over a cliff.' This is a true statement," he announced. "Take them out and execute them," he said to the chief guard.

The guards began to escort the party to the door, but the chief guard stopped after only a few steps. "Uh . . . Chief Justice?" he said timidly.

"Yes."

"Uh . . . how should we execute them?"

"What do you mean, how?"

"Should we feed them to a Smorg or throw them over a cliff?"

"Throw them over a cliff, of course," barked the Chief Justice, annoyed.

"Uh . . . but Chief Justice. That's what she *said* we would do. So her statement is *true*. For true statements, don't we have to feed them to a Smorg?"

The Chief Justice raised his eyebrows. "I suppose you're right, at that." He paused. "Okay, so feed them to a Smorg," he ordered.

"Uh . . . I'm not very smart, so you'll have to forgive me. But if we feed them to a Smorg, then the girl's statement is *false*. She said they would be thrown over a cliff. For false statements we have to throw them over a cliff. And you just said that we couldn't do that, because then her statement is *true*, in which case we would have to feed them to a Smorg—which we can't do because then her statement is false." The guard looked at the Chief Justice helplessly, scratching his head.

The Chief Justice frowned and began thinking about the problem. The girl *had* made a statement as required. And although the truth or falsehood of the statement flipped every time they tried to carry out the execution, one could easily tell if it was true or false as he had specified. He had to admit that the statement met all of the rules he had given them.

And yet it left them with no way to execute the three prisoners.

The girl had outsmarted them.

The crowd looked on intently. What would the Chief Justice do now? This was a contest that would live on in history. The room was deathly silent.

Suddenly, the Chief Justice began laughing. His laughter continued for a very long time before he was able to catch his breath and become serious once again. "These humans," he announced to the crowd, "missed the very last riddle in their Challenge. But by making a statement that completely ties our hands with respect to their mode of execution, they have more than made up for this miss. Unless I hear strong objections from this gathering, by the power of this office, I deem them to be worthy of Mesrobia. And as such, I hereby award them and their Swishmer friend citizenship."

The delighted spectators all stood and began cheering, roaring their approval.

They were free. Jenna grinned from ear to ear. She was glowing so much she was sure that she looked like a neon sign.

This time, it was *she* who had pulled off the miracle.

And it was an incredible feeling.

CHAPTER TWENTY

The Search Continues

Zachary smiled from ear to ear as if a death sentence had just been lifted from his shoulders—which it had been. "You did it Jen!" he exclaimed. "That was *brilliant*. Absolutely *genius!*"

Admiration? From Zachary? Incredible, thought Jenna, beaming.

"Thanks Zack," she said almost shyly.

And then, taking her completely by surprise, her brother hugged her. He actually hugged her. It was a quick hug, but given that she and Zachary had been fighting and teasing each other since they could both talk, it had enormous significance. And then, as if this hadn't been shocking enough, seconds later both she and Zachary were hugging Lisgar, who drew them close with her antennae; her affection for the humans unmistakable. She was cool to the touch, and while her red exoskeleton looked to be as hard and smooth as shell, thousands of nearly invisible hairs covered her body, so she was far softer than they had expected.

Incredible. Hugging an enormous wasp, whose appearance was far more terrifying than anything Jenna had ever conjured up in her worst nightmares, was not exactly something she thought she would ever be doing. And yet, it felt natural.

"I can never thank you enough," said Lisgar, radiating joy. "I wish there was something I could do to repay you."

"You don't owe us anything," said Zachary softly, and Jenna nodded her agreement beside him. Both were surprised at the remarkable level of affection they had developed for Lisgar in such a short time. After having to fight for their lives seemingly every second since they had gone through the first portal, having a companion who was kind, gentle and understanding had been more important than they could ever have guessed. In fact, she reminded them a little of their own mom, and given her appearance, this was saying quite a lot.

"We're just glad we could help you get back to your family," said Jenna. "You've been wonderful to us, and I'm sure you're the same way with your own kids."

As she said it, Jenna realized just how awesome her own parents were, and that she had taken them for granted far more than she should have. She vowed that this would change if they were ever reunited. The possibility that she would never see her parents continued to be more frightening than anything she and her brother had gone through since leaving their kitchen.

Lisgar bent over and squeezed Jenna tightly, holding the hug for a long, long time. "Don't despair," she said softly, guessing exactly what Jenna had been thinking. "You'll find your parents. I just know it. After watching you and your brother together, I know that *nothing* can stop you." She paused. "And when you do find your parents, tell them for me that I think their children are very, very special—although I'm sure they already know that."

Lisgar's kind words could not have been more gratifying to Jenna. She had always been so sure that her parents were disappointed in her. Maybe this was something she needed to reconsider if her life ever got back to normal. They were always telling her they were proud of her. Maybe she should start believing them a little.

The crowd was still producing a loud roar of excited conversation. The Chief Justice had let the three new citizens embrace and celebrate for a few minutes but finally interrupted them. "The portal back to Lisgar's world will be appearing about three miles from here in just a short while and it won't stick around long. If she misses it she won't have another chance for two weeks."

The Chief Justice instructed a guard to lead Lisgar to the portal. After a warm goodbye to her human friends and one last wave at the door, she was on her way.

It took nearly an hour for the crowd to clear the building. They stood in line, everyone wanting a chance to talk to the two humans. Finally the crowd was gone and they were alone with the Chief Justice, now their friend. The Challenge and its aftermath had been exhilarating, but it was nice to finally have a little quiet and calm in the room.

"I have news," the Chief Justice announced to them after everyone had left. "It seems my answer to your question, Jenna, was incorrect. One of my men approached me after the contest to tell me that he had seen an adult man and woman of your species on Mesrobia. Just a few weeks ago."

"Fantastic!" said Jenna. *These had to have been their parents*. "Are they still on Mesrobia?" she asked eagerly.

"No. In fact, the reason no one bothered to report this to me is that they were here for only a minute or two. There is a group of four portals, right next to each other, a short walk from here. Apparently, the humans were seen from a distance arriving through one of the portals, and then immediately leaving through another."

"Does the man who told you this know which one they left through?" asked Zachary.

"I'm afraid not. It happened too quickly. But it was definitely one of those four."

"Can you take us there?" said Jenna.

"I'd be glad to," replied the Chief Justice. "Follow me."

While they walked, the two humans told the Chief Justice about the arrival of the first portal in their kitchen that had swallowed up their parents, and how they had come to be on Mesrobia. "You seem to know everything about the portals," said Zachary. "Now that we're citizens, can you tell us their secret? And how we can get back home once we find our parents?"

The Chief Justice frowned and stopped walking. "Well . . . about knowing everything about the portals," he began, looking guilty. "We act like we do. We tell the visitors we invite here that we do. But the truth is that we really don't know that much. Mesrobia is connected by portals to so many other worlds that we need to protect ourselves. If these other worlds all think we have knowledge of the portals they don't have, and can use this knowledge to our advantage, they'll think twice before trying to attack us."

Zachary's heart fell. He could understand why the Mesrobians pretended to know more than they did, but he had been so hopeful they would finally be getting some answers. "But I thought you said if we passed the test you could return us to our world."

"I can return you to the world you came here from. But that's all. I just assumed you came here from your own world."

"Is there anything you can tell us about the portals?" asked Jenna.

"Not a lot. We know that they're all the same size. We know some are stable, while many appear and reappear at regular intervals. And that most of them are one way.

Notice that after you arrive on a new world, the portal isn't usually still open behind you for the return trip. The portal that Lisgar will take back to her world is not in the same location as the one that brought her here."

"What causes the portals to exist in the first place?" asked Zachary. "Magic?"

The Chief Justice laughed. "I guess that's as good an explanation as any. I have no idea. What causes the sun to exist? Maybe that's magic too."

"Is there any way to control them?" said Zachary. "To spring them open where you want?"

"Not as far as I know. If you're suggesting someone controlled a portal so it would appear under your parents, on purpose, I highly doubt it."

Zachary frowned. As time went on it seemed they were getting further away from solving this puzzle rather than closer.

They finally arrived at their destination, a small, pyramid-shaped building. There was nothing inside except the four active portals the Chief Justice had described. The kids examined each of the four. They looked through the first and were greeted by a blizzard raging across a barren arctic landscape. It looked colder and less inviting even than the North Pole. They were unable to see through the next two portals at all, which the Chief Justice said was sometimes the case. The final portal was a window on an arid desert without any signs of life as far as they could see.

"Which one will you take?" asked an interested Chief Justice.

Zachary raised his eyebrows. "Well, the ones we can see through give us a choice of freezing to death or getting baked to death," he said. "My parents would have taken one of the middle two, that's for sure."

Jenna nodded her agreement.

Zachary turned to her. "Your choice, Jen," he said. "You've earned it."

This was a small gesture, but the respect behind it was huge. Pride swelled up inside of her. There was no difference between the second and third portals, but ever since she could remember she had a fondness for the number three. Perhaps it would be lucky. She pointed at the third portal. "Let's try this one," she said.

It promptly disappeared, almost as if on cue.

The Chief Justice frowned at the portal's bad timing. "It will return in about ten minutes," he said reassuringly. "Unfortunately, I have to leave now. Just wait here until it returns." He met Zachary's gaze. "But before I go, I want you to know that I will honor your request and find a way to change the trespassing law so that it works but doesn't punish the innocent." He paused. "And thanks. Thanks for providing the kick in the pants I needed to do what I should have done in the first place."

He took two steps back from the humans. "I know that you have to try to find your parents without delay," he said. "Which is very much a shame. We would have loved for you to stay here for a while. You two are very, very impressive. Naturally, as Mesrobian citizens, you will always be welcome here." He looked at them warmly. "Good luck to you both."

"Thank you," said the two humans together as the Chief Justice exited the building, leaving them alone to await the return of the portal.

Their mood was the best it had been in a long time. Their parents had been seen alive fairly recently, and if they got lucky and chose the right portal, they might be right on their parents' heels. Things could have been better, but they also could have been a lot worse.

"While we're waiting," said Jenna, "any new ideas as to what's going on? Or what the worlds we've visited might have in common?"

Zachary paused in thought before finally shaking his head. "None. Each world has different types of civilizations. They all have different numbers of portals. And the natives all have different levels of knowledge about them."

"Yeah. That about sums it up," said Jenna dejectedly.

"There is one thing they all have in common, of course."

Jenna regarded him quizzically.

"The air," he said simply.

"The air?"

Zachary nodded. "You know, the atmosphere. Oxygen and nitrogen—like on Earth. I mean, there are planets in our solar system with poison atmospheres that would kill us in minutes. Some planets don't have *any* atmosphere."

Jenna gulped. "Thanks for reminding me. As if I don't have enough to worry about when I go through a portal."

"And then there's gravity," continued Zachary. "The gravity on all the worlds we've been on so far is almost exactly the same as Earth's. Which is good. Because as cool as it would be to land on a planet as small as the Moon—where we could jump six times farther than we're used to—if we landed on a planet like Jupiter, its gravity would instantly squash us into *paste*." He looked ill as he imagined this fate. "And then there are planets that are thousands of degrees hot. Or have deadly radiation. Or are totally volcanic. Or are— "

"Okay, okay," snapped Jenna. "I get the point! There are all kinds of ways for us to die horribly the instant we step through a portal. *I get it*."

Zachary scrunched up his face. "Sorry," he said meekly. "I'll stop now."

He paused in thought. "You know," he said, his voice now taking on a guarded enthusiasm, "I'll bet the portals can only open between worlds that can support our type of life. I mean, so far that's been the case."

"You're just saying that to make me feel better."

"Well, yeah, but the more I think about it, the more sure I am that it's true. I mean, it hasn't just been true for us, but for Mom and Dad also."

Jenna brightened. "Good point. And they've been on a lot more worlds than we have."

"Exactly."

"And if there were portals that led to instant death, the Chief Justice would have mentioned it, right?"

"Right," said Zachary. He frowned and added, "Although I wish I would have thought to ask him that."

They stood in silence for several long seconds. "We're not getting anywhere, are we?" said Zachary.

Jenna shook her head and then shrugged. "How do you solve a puzzle when all of the pieces are totally unrelated?"

"Good question," said Zachary miserably. "I only wish I had a good answer."

As he finished speaking, the portal Jenna had chosen suddenly reappeared in front of them.

Jenna eyed it warily. "Should we go through?"

Zachary nodded, and then sighed deeply. "Maybe we'll find some answers on the next world."

Jenna took her brother's hand and looked down at the shimmering portal. What would await them on the other side? Their parents? Some answers? Or maybe a planet full of poisonous air.

"On three," said Zachary, still holding his sister's hand.

They closed their eyes as had become their custom. "One, two, three," they said as they took a small jump forward into the center of the portal.

They felt an all too familiar sensation and then firm ground under their feet. The climate was slightly damp and on the chilly side, but reasonably pleasant.

They opened their eyes.

And saw nothing. *And saw nothing.*

They gasped in horror.

They were completely blind.

CHAPTER TWENTY-ONE

Tentacles

They closed their eyes tightly and then reopened them.

There was no difference. It was totally, completely, black either way.

Jenna was still holding her brother's hand. She clutched at it for reassurance. She held her other hand up an inch from her eyes. She couldn't see it at all.

"Zack," she whispered in panic, "where are we?"

"I don't know," Zachary whispered back, his voice distraught.

Even on the darkest, blackest night there was *some* light. Here they were on a strange world—undoubtedly a dangerous one—and they couldn't see a thing. Without being able to see they were utterly helpless.

Their imaginations ran wild. Who could guess what vicious predator was even now licking its chops, drool running over its fangs, moments away from pouncing. And they had thought a giant wasp had been frightening.

That was child's play compared to this. Nothing could generate the raw, primal fear of being in an unknown and likely dangerous place and not being able to see. Their hearts beat so hard against their chests they thought they might burst.

"Take hold of my waist," croaked Zachary, fighting to control his panic. He heard a hollow echo as he spoke. "I'm gonna start moving."

When he felt his sister's hands around his waist he put his arms out in front of him and began to shuffle forward, only inches at a time, having no way to tell if he was an inch away from slamming into a dangerous obstacle or falling over the edge of a cliff. Years before he had closed his eyes and tried to walk around his house, just to get an idea of what it was like to be blind. Even pretending he had only been able to do so for a few minutes before it had freaked him out so much that he just had to open his eyes.

His hand hit something hard. He jerked it back.

He let out a sigh of relief. It was only a rock wall of some kind, smooth and cool to the touch. He put both hands out and moved them up, down, and sideways along the wall. "I think we're in a cave," he said finally. "Do you hear the hollow echo?"

Jenna nodded, not remembering that he couldn't see her. "I think you're right. No wonder it's so dark."

"We have to find a way out of here," said Zachary. He continued walking cautiously, sliding his left hand forward along the wall as a guide. "We won't survive for long if we don't."

Jenna held his waist and followed as he focused all of his concentration on moving forward. With her other hand she reached into her pocket and removed the small generator Zachary had given her and held it. For some reason, its presence in her hand was reassuring—at least a little. And in her state of almost total terror, she needed all the reassurance she could get.

Visions of fanged alien bats, or worse, flying toward their necks or sneaking up on them continued to torture their imaginations. Only their sense of hearing could now alert them to any threats, but strain as they might they could only hear the sound of their own shuffling and the thunderous pounding of their hearts.

Slide—stop. Slide—stop. Slide—stop. Their progress was painfully slow.

They had been moving in this way for about twenty minutes—which seemed like twenty hours—when they detected a glow, ever so faint, in the distance. After another few minutes of slow progress they made their way to its source. It gradually came into focus.

It was a tree. A miniature tree not more than five feet tall. It had a full complement of tiny white branches with delicate, perfectly formed transparent leaves, outlined in silver along their edges. The leaves were shaped like butterfly wings and were the size of one of Jenna's fingernails. Somehow, each of the leaves glowed from within, ever so slightly, providing just the barest hint of illumination. The glow was so faint that even against total darkness the entire tree full of the leaves, spread out as they were, only provided illumination enough for them to see a few feet in front of them. But after total darkness even the faintest light was a relief.

Jenna reached out and touched a branch gently. The tiny, faintly glowing leaves shimmered as she did so. "It's beautiful," she whispered admiringly.

Zachary didn't respond. Instead, he took a few steps away from the tree and peered ahead in the distance where he could just barely make out a number of discrete glows within a few yards of each other. "I think there are about ten more of these . . . Glow-trees . . . farther ahead," he announced excitedly. If these trees grew throughout the cave, they might be able to find an exit after all. "Let's make our way over— "

Zachary grunted as if he'd been hit in the stomach.

"Zack?" cried Jenna, looking up quickly. In the dim glow she could just make out her brother. A huge tentacle was wrapped tightly around his stomach and he had been lifted off the ground. The tentacle was covered with suction cups and was attached to a hideous creature that she could barely see since it was almost entirely out of the range of the Glow-tree and facing away from the dim light. She could just make out that it was pale and hairless. Two huge oval eyes, without lids, bulged out from its face like the eyes of a praying mantis. It was repulsive.

Jenna opened her mouth to scream.

Before she was even aware it had moved, the creature whipped the second of its two tentacle arms around her waist, taking her breath away. It lifted her off her feet, still facing away from the Glow-tree, and ran off with her and her brother on human-like legs.

They were instantly plunged back into the absolute darkness of the cave, the only illumination coming from the creature's massive, bulging eyes as they continued to gleam demonically. From the surefooted manner that the creature ran it was clear that its eyes were thousands of times more sensitive than theirs, gathering and magnifying light they couldn't possibly have detected.

Zachary felt the tentacle that was holding Jenna brush up against him as the creature ran. Grunting, he kicked at it with all his might.

And it let go.

Surprised, the creature recoiled slightly, just enough to lose its grip on Jenna. She fell to the cave floor. It whipped another tentacle out to try to pick her up again but missed, hitting her arm in the process and sending the small Omega field generator flying from her hand. The plastic ball bounced along the cave floor and then fell thirty feet to the bottom of a cavern, making a distant cracking noise as it landed.

"No!" screamed Jenna, even as she jerked to the left, blindly dodging a tentacle she was sure would make another attempt to seize her.

Zachary pounded on the tentacle coiled around him and used all of his strength to try to squirm away from the monster. Anything to distract it from his sister.

The creature was determined not to let him get away. It wrapped its other tentacle around Zachary's arms and continued into the darkness, leaving Jenna behind.

"Zack!" she screamed in horror. "Where are you!"

But there was no answer. All she could hear was the sound of the creature's running footsteps for another fifteen seconds—and then nothing.

Her brother was gone.

And so was the generator that had helped her so much.

She crumpled onto the cave floor in despair.

She was alone. In total silence—and total darkness. She could barely breathe, as if she had been hit hard in the stomach by a steel fist.

Jenna curled up into a ball on the ground, too emotionally numb even to sob as she plunged into depths of despair she didn't even know existed. Totally stunned, she made no move to lift herself off the cave floor. This had to be a nightmare. Just a nightmare. She would wake up any moment.

Just then she saw the blackness shimmer only inches away. It couldn't be. Was she imagining it?

She sat up and fought to recover her emotional balance. *It was a portal.* She looked through it and saw daylight. After the total darkness of the cave the daylight was painful, far too bright to take, and she instinctively slammed her eyes shut to protect them. She re-opened her eyes just a fraction and squinted through the portal until they adjusted.

And then something remarkable happened as she looked through the portal.

Her parents appeared.

Her mom and dad—clear as day. *They were alive*. Not ten feet from her through the portal.

"Mom! Dad!" she gasped in wonder. Her spirits soared. Just for a moment she forgot where she was and the danger she was in.

But only for a moment. A picture of the hideous creature that now had her brother popped back into her mind. "You have to help me. Something has Zachary!"

Tears welled up in her mother's eyes. "Jenna!" she said in disbelief, gazing lovingly at her daughter. "Is that really you?" Her voice sounded incredibly distant filtered through the portal. She turned toward her husband. "You did it! You thought you could direct this portal to the kids and you were right!"

"But I can only keep it open for a few minutes," said Mr. Lane, the strain in his voice unmistakable. He turned his full attention to his daughter. "Are you okay, Jenna?" he asked protectively.

"I'm okay," she replied. "But Zack's in big trouble. We've got to help him."

Her parents looked confused and concerned. "It looks like you're saying something, Jenna, but we can't hear a thing. You're going to have to speak louder. Where is your brother?"

"*He was kidnapped*," she yelled at the top of her lungs. "*By some hideous cave monster.*"

"We can't hear you," said her father worriedly. "Can you hear *us*? If you can hear me, wave your hands in front of you," he instructed.

Jenna did as he requested.

"Good," said her mother, looking relieved. "At least you can hear *us*. You're going to have to jump through the portal to us, Sweetheart. I promise you everything will be okay."

"But Zachary," pleaded Jenna again. "You don't understand. We have to help him."

Jenna gasped as she noticed the portal beginning to shrink ever so slightly.

"We still can't hear you, Sweetheart," said her father urgently, panic creeping into his voice. "But the portal is beginning to shrink. You don't have much time. Jump through now!" he insisted. "Please! This portal won't return for a hundred years. And I won't be able to create an opening between us again."

What should she do? She looked at her parent's kind, worried faces. Their eyes were pleading with her to join them. In seconds she could be in their arms and away from this endless darkness. Away from this terrible nightmare. They always knew what to do. They would take care of her.

She looked at them longingly. These were the parents who had read stories to her and tucked her in at night. Who had comforted her when she was sick. Who had dried her tears when she was hurt; physically or emotionally. They had always been there for her.

And they were there for her now. Just a single step away.

She loved them so much. And she needed them desperately.

But her brother needed *her*. Now. He didn't stand a chance against the tentacled monstrosity that had captured him. She couldn't just leave him. She had never realized until this moment how much she loved her brother. But she did. Deeply. The intensity of her emotions surprised her.

And she was hit with the realization that he must love her too. Hadn't he stayed behind with her to face the deadly Grull. He could have made it through the portal to safety when the Grull had been chasing them. But he had slowed on purpose when he realized *she* wouldn't make it. He told her he hadn't, but she knew better. Yes, he could be a huge jerk. Yes, he was always putting her down. But when she had needed him most, when it *mattered* most, he had refused to leave her side, even when he knew they had almost no hope of survival.

And she could do no less for him. She would save her brother. She just *had* to. Somehow.

But it seemed so hopeless. The enemy was much stronger than she was and had super-sensitive vision. She was a weak, blind girl against a sighted, impossibly strong creature. And there were no weapons here. Even if she found a weapon she couldn't see to use it.

But they had been in impossible situations before—and gotten out of them. She had never thought so clearly or been so sure of herself.

But that was only because she was carrying her parents miracle generator, she realized, which had been performing its own brand of magic. Without it, she was just as pathetic as she had always been.

What would Zachary do in this situation? she asked herself. The answer came to her quickly. He would find a way to trick the creature or outsmart it. He would find a way to use the creature's advantages against it. He had done this with the Grull when he had tricked it into using its own cruel impulses to unwittingly set them free.

She had to think of *something*. Even without the generator. She couldn't just leave her brother here with that monster.

The portal was now only seconds away from closing.

"*Please*, Jenna! Please come through now," pleaded her mother.

Several tears escaped from Jenna's eyes and rolled slowly down her face. "I love you both," she said sadly, despite knowing they couldn't hear her. "But I won't leave Zachary," she whispered.

With that, the portal disappeared and plunged her once again into a thick blanket of darkness.

Jenna forced herself to turn away from where the now-vanished portal, and her parents, had been. She had made her choice. Finding a strength within herself that she didn't know existed, she defiantly wiped away her tears and rose to her feet. She made a determined fist. If there was a way—*any* way—to free her brother, she told herself, she would find it.

But despite her resolve, she knew that her chance of success was as close to zero as it could possibly get.

CHAPTER TWENTY-TWO

Darkness

After a few minutes of running the creature stopped and began walking slowly, even cautiously, for several minutes. Finally, it stopped and set Zachary down on the cool cave floor, its tentacles still wrapped around him. "I'm going to let go," it said. "But you should know you have no chance of escape."

It could talk? It was intelligent?

Zachary realized he shouldn't have been surprised. After Tular, the Grull, and especially Lisgar, he should have known just how deceiving appearances could be.

"We're standing on a natural rock bridge high over a cavern. I was observing you for several minutes and it's obvious you're blind. So don't even think of trying to escape. Take one wrong step and you'll plunge to your death. I'd hate for that to happen before I'm finished with you."

Me too, thought Zachary, but he remained silent as the creature's tentacles uncoiled from around him and he took a deep breath, freed from their crushing hold.

"Now," roared the alien, "tell me how to get home!"

"How to get home?" repeated Zachary in confusion.

"Don't play stupid. I don't know how you arranged to bring me here, but I want to go back."

"I don't understand. I thought this *was* your home. How did you get here?"

"As if you don't know," snorted the creature. "I was on a hunting expedition in my home cave when I stumbled into some kind of bizarre hole. The next thing I knew I was on this world." It reached out with a tentacle and shook Zachary roughly. "Now send me back right now!"

Zachary was intrigued. This alien had travelled through a portal. It . . . he . . . had gone from one cave world to another. "How do you know you're not just in a different section of the cave you were in when you fell?" asked Zachary. "What makes you think you're in an entirely different world?"

"How stupid do you take me for? Everything is different. The rock formations, the animals, the bats—those stupid trees. Everything." He glared at Zachary. "We both know this isn't my world. Now why have your kind brought me here?"

"Look," said Zachary. "I understand why you're upset. But this is all a big mistake. My name is Zachary. I'm a human. I'm not from here either. I got here the same way you did."

The creature snorted. "You can't expect me to fall for that one," he said. "You were obviously coming to attack me."

Zachary's mouth fell open. "To attack you!" he repeated in dismay. "*You?* Are you kidding? Look at me! Do I look like I belong in a cave? I can't see one inch in front of my face. I couldn't successfully attack a fuzzy *caterpillar*."

The creature paused for a long moment in thought. "What you say seems to make sense. But it must be a trick," he said stubbornly. "You and your companion do seem totally helpless. But maybe you're trying to get me overconfident—so I lower my guard."

"My companion, as you call her, is my sister. And we're both just kids. More importantly, we're in the exact same boat as you. Really. You have to believe me. I'm just as much of a stranger here as you are."

"I think it's more likely that you and your sister—if that's really who she is—were sent to study me. To learn the physical weaknesses of my kind. Perhaps your people are preparing to start a war with mine."

"How were we sent here to study you? If you hadn't attacked us, we would never have been able to even *find* you. Do you think we tricked you into attacking us?"

"You are very good with words, but you still won't fool me."

Zachary groaned. He was getting nowhere. Maybe he should try to establish some common ground as a basis for trust. He asked his captor for his name.

"I am Nivek. That is all I will tell you. Now, I will ask again—how can I get back home?"

"I really don't know," whispered Zachary in frustration.

Nivek nodded. "Let's see if a few weeks without food doesn't cause you to change your story."

Zachary frowned deeply. This Nivek was the most suspicious creature he had ever met. What would make somebody so paranoid that he wouldn't listen to reason?

And then Zachary remembered Tular. His world had been impossibly hostile. Even the most innocent looking creatures were deadly. That was the only world Tular had ever known. If they hadn't saved Tular's life, would he have ever trusted them? Probably not. The experience of a lifetime had taught him not to trust any creature that wasn't a Krug.

"Is every creature hostile and deadly on your world?" asked Zachary.

"What?" said Nivek in disbelief. "Of course. How could it be otherwise?"

Zachary nodded. At least now he knew what he was up against. Nivek had good reason not to trust him. He had to find a way to open his mind to the idea that worlds existed on which creatures from different species cooperated, or at the very least left each other in peace.

Zachary thought about it longer, and decided that convincing the alien to trust him over the next few days was his only chance. Even if he could escape, which would take a miracle, without being able to see he was as good as dead. Nivek had said everything on this world was different than on his: including the native animals. This had confirmed Zachary's worst fear: there were definitely bats and other creatures in this cave. He and Jenna just hadn't run across any yet.

"Jenna!" he whispered in horror.

He had been relieved when he had caused Nivek to release her, thinking he had saved her from certain death. But just the *opposite* was true.

He suddenly found it impossible to breathe as fear for his sister constricted his throat like a massive python.

He could count on protection from Nivek, at least for now, but Jenna was alone and helpless. He pictured a living sea of alien bats descending on her like fanged locusts, tearing her to ribbons. The vision was so real he almost collapsed to the ground in grief. "We have to go back for my sister," he croaked. "Right now!"

"Oh really? And why is that?"

"Because she's totally *helpless*. She's at the mercy of the bats and other cave creatures." The absolute panic in his voice was unmistakable. "*Please*. I'm *begging* you. We have to go back for her."

"Nice performance," said Nivek with a smirk. "But you don't think you can lead me into a trap that easily, do you? You know as well as I do that there aren't any bats or other animals within ten miles of here. They all live near the cave entrance."

Zachary's eyes lit up. Nivek was telling the truth. He was sure of it. Which meant that Jenna was definitely still alive, and in no immediate danger. Right now she was probably travelling the relatively short distance back to the Glow-tree they had been near when Nivek had snatched them.

Zachary's suffocating panic melted away, and he took a deep, relieved breath. "That's fantastic!" he said. "But I *didn't* know that. I don't have any idea where I am, or where the entrance is. My sister and I arrived here just like you did, very close to where you found us."

Nivek didn't respond.

The cave became utterly silent, making the darkness even more unsettling. Zachary knew he had to find a way to gradually open Nivek's mind to the idea that he wasn't dangerous and didn't mean him any harm. He began to describe Earth, and everything he and Jenna had gone through since the portal had first appeared under their parents. After several hours of this, he was finally able to get Nivek to open up a little also. Nivek passionately described his home world and Zachary grew to believe that he was probably a decent . . . being. Zachary felt sorry for him. Nivek hadn't asked to fall through the portal and leave his world, and everyone and everything he knew, behind. If anyone could understand what he was going through, Zachary could.

Finally, Nivek announced that he would be taking a nap. Although he was slightly less suspicious than he had been, Zachary knew he still had a long way to go to gain the alien's trust.

Zachary heard his captor sit down against the cave wall at the end of the rock bridge. The location of Nivek's gleaming eyes changed also, verifying his position. His eyes were all that Zachary could see—and only then just barely.

"Remember," said Nivek. "I'm a light sleeper. So don't think for a second you can grope your way across the bridge before I wake up. You don't have a chance."

"Don't worry. I'm not going anywhere. Enjoy your nap."

Nivek's breathing became regular and he was soon asleep.

Zachary had been fascinated by Nivek's ability to see clearly in the dark and during their discussion he had learned why the cave dweller didn't have any eyelids. His eyes were always open, even during sleep. Not only did they gather light, like a telescope, but they also stored it, like a battery. This was the reason they glowed faintly. Zachary couldn't even imagine what it would be like to sleep with his eyes open.

As Nivek slept, Zachary continued thinking about how to convince him he was friendly, trying to ignore the ocean of darkness and the sound of his own heart pounding far more loudly in his ears than should have been possible.

The absolute darkness was suffocating his spirit. It would be such a relief to see again. *Anything.* Just to believe he still could. Perhaps the faint light given off by Nivek's eyes would be enough. His own eyes had adjusted as much as human eyes could to the dark, and would now pick up light with greater sensitivity than ever before.

He took out the purple crystal in his pocket—the language transformer that had served them so well. Perhaps the small amount of light would reflect off its glassy surface and be amplified. If he could only see the crystal, at least this would be a start. He strained as hard as he could, but he couldn't see it, even when he held it just a few inches from his face.

He continued staring at the crystal in his hand, as though through the power of his will alone he could force his eyes to see it.

Zachary gasped as an image appeared in his head. Not of the crystal, but of him and Nivek in the cave, as though seen from above and in perfect lighting.

The scene disappeared an instant later.

Had it even been real? Or was his desire to be able to see so strong that his mind had fooled itself into believing he could see the entire area, and even himself? As if he were having an out-of-body experience.

He tried to capture the image in his head once again, but failed. He could bring back its memory, but the memory was just the shadow of the crisp image that had appeared for just a fraction of a second. Or at least that he *thought* had appeared. But maybe not. Darkness and fear were probably driving him mad.

He heard a faint shuffle in the distance. *What was that?* His mind was playing even more tricks on him.

No, there it was again.

A chill shot up his spine. Nivek had said there were no other creatures in this part of the cave. Was he wrong, after all? Should Zachary awaken him for protection? Or was his mind snapping like a dry twig under the strain and the darkness.

Zachary strained to see, but of course it did him no good. But wait. Now he *could* see something. A faint halo of light coming closer. Light?

Closer. Closer.

It was Jenna.

She was slowly, stealthily, walking across the narrow stone bridge.

He stifled a gasp. She was trying to rescue him. And it was her hair that was glowing.

Her hair?

And then he realized what she had done. She had crushed hundreds of the tiny glowing leaves from the miniature trees they had discovered and put them in her hair. Her hair glowed ever so faintly, just enough so she could see a few feet in front of her.

She was barefoot so she would make less noise. One tennis shoe was tied by its laces around her waist and the other was tied like a necklace around her neck. A sock was stuffed inside the shoe hanging from her neck, and the end of the sock brushed against her chin. She wore an expression of total concentration and determination.

Jenna had come back for him. What bravery.

When she was a few yards closer he would be able to see well enough to move toward her, and together they could return to the other side of the bridge. With the light from her hair guiding the way, they could escape Nivek and attempt to find a way out of the cave. Zachary held his breath as she moved steadily closer.

Nivek bolted awake.

One moment Zachary heard him rise and the next he saw him on the bridge, outlined in his sister's faintly glowing halo, with both tentacles wrapped tightly around her. He was amazingly quick. Turning his face away from Jenna, Nivek used the tip of one of his tentacles to quickly rub her hair until all of the leaves fell out, once again leaving them in total darkness.

"Is this sneak attack an example of how I can trust you, Zachary the Human?" he growled. "This is proof of your treachery. She is here to kill me in my sleep. And just when I was starting to believe you when you said you meant me no harm."

"But you don't understand—" began Zachary.

"Silence!" roared Nivek in fury. "No more talk. You've both just signed your death warrants!" he said with finality.

CHAPTER TWENTY-THREE

Light

"I don't think so," said Jenna defiantly.

Nivek had a firm grip around her arms, but in one quick motion she lowered her chin and clamped her teeth onto the sock that was stuffed into her shoe. She yanked her head back, pulling the sock plug completely out. Inside the shoe she had crammed thousands upon thousands of tiny leaves, collected from dozens of Glow-trees, and their combined glow produced the illumination of a dim light bulb.

Nivek screamed in agony.

The sudden light was painful to the humans, but to Nivek, a being whose eyes were thousands of times more sensitive to light, the brightness was blinding, overloading his eyes and causing searing pain. Worse still, the alien didn't have any eyelids to close to protect his eyes. He let go of Jenna and dived backwards to get away from the light.

And he missed the bridge.

He began plummeting toward the cavern floor far below. He was just able to reach up as he fell and grab onto the bridge with four suction cups on the very tip of one of his tentacles. He continued moaning in pain, even as he struggled to cling to the bridge.

Jenna looked down at the struggling creature triumphantly. *She had done it*. She had defeated this monster. She had found the one weapon that wasn't effective against a blind person but was very effective against a creature who could see: a bright, blinding light in the eyes. She had figured out how to turn the creature's strength—its vastly superior night-vision—against it. She had *wanted* it to catch her. That was part of her plan. She needed it to be close enough so the surprise package of light in her shoe would have its maximum effect.

And it had. She had sprung her trap flawlessly.

The creature was at their mercy now. Two of the four suction cups holding it on had come free with a loud pop. In only seconds now it would complete its fall.

As soon as Zachary's eyes adjusted to the light coming from his sister's shoe he dashed forward and knelt down on the bridge above where Nivek was clinging.

"What are you doing?" said Jenna. "Come on Zack! Get up and let's go!"

He ignored her. Instead, Jenna watched in disbelief as her brother reached down and grabbed the thing's tentacled arm and pulled with all his strength.

"Jen, help me!" he shouted. "Quick! We have to save him!"

Jenna's eyes widened in shock. *Zachary wanted the creature saved? The same creature that had promised to kill them?*

"Jenna!" yelled Zachary. "*Hurry!*"

Jenna knew she had no time for questions. She had to trust her brother. She quickly bent down to help him. Together they were able to pull Nivek enough of the way up that he could reach up with his other tentacle and pull himself the rest of the way onto the bridge.

He laid on the ledge, panting from exertion, as Zachary hastily removed Jenna's shoe from around her neck and covered the opening with his hand to block the light.

"Are you okay?" asked Zachary.

Still grimacing in pain, Nivek nodded. There was a long silence as he regained his breath. "Your sister's weapon blinded me. I don't know if I'll ever see again." His eyes had absorbed a considerable amount of light and were glowing more brightly than ever.

"Yeah, well, sorry about that," said Jenna, not sounding at all sorry. "But you attacked *us*. And I thought you meant to hurt my brother."

"Actually . . . I did," admitted Nivek. "I can't blame you for what you did. And I'm the one who's sorry. Your brother saved my life," he said in amazement. "After I kidnapped and threatened him. I never would have believed it. He was being honest after all. You are *not* my enemies." Nivek paused. "Thank you, Zachary the Human."

"You're very welcome," said Zachary with a smile. "Jenna—meet Nivek. He's from a cave world and came here by accident. His world is like Tular's; extremely dangerous. He isn't really a bad . . . guy. He just thought we were out to get him."

"I'm sorry for what I did to you and your brother, Jenna," said Nivek. "On my world we learn from a very young age that *everything* is dangerous. But this isn't my world. I should have taken that into account."

Zachary nodded. They had somehow managed to dodge yet another bullet. "Well, now that we're past that awkward stage of our relationship—you know, where we both try to kill each other—maybe we can work together."

Nivek agreed.

Zachary considered what to do from here. Nivek needed total darkness again if he was to fully recover—if a full recovery was even possible. Zachary was still blocking the light from exiting Jenna's shoe with his hand, but he had had more than enough of total darkness.

"Nivek," he said, "I have an idea. I need to talk to my sister, and you need to recover in total darkness. So I think we should take our Glow leaves into the next section of cave for a while. We'll come back in an hour to see how your recovery is going. Would that be okay?"

"That is a wise idea, Zachary. The farther those leaves are away from me, the better, as you guessed." He paused. "And Jenna the Human, congratulations for defeating me in battle. I had never before imagined that so much light could be stored in such a small space. The power of your shoe-weapon was astonishing. And your strategy of using yourself as bait to draw me close was truly impressive. You are almost totally helpless physically, and yet you beat me. Because of this, you should know you are the finest warrior I have ever known."

"Uh . . . thanks, Nivek," she responded awkwardly. She had been called many things in her life, but warrior had never been one of them.

Zachary and Jenna moved away into the adjacent section of the cave and huddled around Jenna's shoe, which gave off enough light for them to see each other at close quarters.

If Nivek had been impressed with Jenna, her brother was even *more* impressed. He praised her profusely for the extraordinary courage she had shown coming to his rescue. And for her strategy. "Jenna, that was brilliant," he said. "*Beyond* brilliant."

Jenna didn't seem to be reacting to his praise the way he thought she would. In fact, she looked miserable, although he couldn't be absolutely certain in the dim light. "Jenna, is everything okay?" he whispered. He forced a smile. "I mean, you do get that I've been giving you compliments and not insults, right?"

"Zack," she whispered back, her voice filled with anguish. "I lost the generator."

"The *what?*" said Zachary.

"Mom and Dad's generator. The one that makes you stronger and smarter. I lost it forever. So I wasn't brilliant," she said. "I was lucky. Like when I play Boggle against you. When the portal opened to Mom and Dad, the light hurt my eyes, which is what gave me the idea. Any idiot could have figured it out from there."

"Portal to Mom and Dad! *What are you talking about?*"

Jenna realized that this should have been the first thing she told her brother. She began describing what had happened, and as she talked about seeing her parents and watching the portal close, she looked to be in as much emotional agony as he had ever seen her in. But her eyes remained dry, as if her hurt was too deep even for tears.

Zachary didn't share this problem. For the first time since they had begun their journey, tears silently streamed down his face and onto the hard cave floor. His sister could have joined their parents. She had been inches away. But she had stayed to try to save him. Her courage had been even more remarkable than he had realized. She had risked everything for a brother who had done nothing but put her down her entire life.

And what kind of universe would allow their luck to be this horrible? If Nivek hadn't captured him—if they had been left alone for even another five minutes—they both would be with their parents right now. *It just wasn't fair*.

Jenna gazed at Zachary in dismay. Her older brother, whom she had never witnessed show emotion in this way, whose tear ducts she hadn't been certain even worked, had finally found something that had broken through his carefully controlled exterior.

She considered trying to cheer him up, but couldn't think of a single positive thing to say. They might never get this close to their parents again. And the deadly danger they faced on each world never seemed to end. "I'm so sorry Zack. But without the generator, I won't be any help at all now. I'm not trying to make you feel bad, but things are worse than ever."

Unexpectedly, this actually helped Zachary get his emotions under control. A new resolve came over his face. "Things are bad," he admitted. "But not worse than ever. At least we're free. And alive. And so are Mom and Dad."

They were both silent for almost a minute. Zachary's face was now completely dry and he was fully himself once again. "And, um . . . about the generator," he said finally through clenched teeth. He looked at Jenna guiltily, but did not continue.

"What about it?"

"Well, I kind of— " He stopped. "I kind of made the whole thing up."

"*You what?*"

"Made the whole thing up. The generator. The Omega field." He shrugged. "All of it. I'm afraid it's not true. There is no such thing."

Jenna looked at her brother, aghast. "But why would you lie to me? Why would you make up that story and spend valuable time on a lie? Why Zack?" she pleaded, clearly hurt.

"I'm sorry, Jen," he said, wincing. "I really am. But you didn't want to come with me. I never knew how little confidence you had in yourself. And everything I told you then was true. You're super quick to get jokes, and you solve problems even better than I do sometimes. And beating me at Boggle isn't lucky, or others would do it every once in a while."

"What does that have to do with lying to me?"

"You were *so* stubborn. I couldn't get you to believe me. And even though you're bright and talented, there's a reason you don't have much confidence. A reason other than that I've been a total jerk to you your entire life."

Jenna stared intently at her brother but did not respond.

"You give up on yourself before you even try. And I knew that if we were gonna save Mom and Dad and survive, I couldn't let that happen. I needed you to be as confident as possible, so you'd be at your best. And you weren't ready to believe in yourself, no matter what I would have said. I had done too much damage over the years. I realized that at the time."

"So what are you saying? That because of this you decided to just make up a fantasy story about a generator? Just for kicks?"

"Not just for kicks. To *help* you. To help *us*. The ball I gave you was from one of Dad's experiments. He was going to throw it out, but I thought it was cool, so he let me keep it. I figured I could use it to fool you into thinking you were carrying a miracle generator. So you would start believing in yourself. Instant self-confidence. I made up all that Omega field stuff as I went along."

"Well, you should be proud," spat Jenna bitterly. "You fooled me. Just like always."

"How can you be mad about this?" said Zachary. "You're missing the big picture, Jen. *It's been all you on these worlds!* That ball you had in your pocket did *nothing*. It just took up space. It didn't help you do amazing things. You did them all on your own."

Jenna's eyes widened. *He was right*. She'd been so intent on learning why he had lied to her she had failed to see the broader implications. She had saved them from crashing into a giant pig on Orum, *all by herself*, and had come up with ideas that had helped them both escape that awful world. No miracle generator had helped her solve riddles on Mesrobia, or find a clever way to avoid an execution. And maybe her plan to free her brother from Nivek wasn't just luck, after all.

Maybe she was too quick to dwell on her faults, and too slow to give herself credit. Maybe she always had been. Like when she had built a laser to win the science fair. Yes, her Dad had helped, but *she* had done most of the work.

By fooling her, her brother had found a way to get the most out of her and open her eyes to her true potential. He had proven to her that she was capable of thinking clearly—all by herself. Without any help. And of thinking quickly and acting boldly under pressure, too.

Zachary watched his sister brighten as the truth exploded upon her.

"You see, Jen. My plan worked. You finally saw what you can do when you have confidence in yourself. If you think you *can't* do something, then you won't try, and you're beat before you start. But even if you aren't naturally good in an area—and no one is great at everything—if you believe you can do something, and you give it all you have, you can do *amazing* things."

"But you *are* great at everything," said Jenna.

"Well, yeah," began Zachary, "I guess that's . . ." He was about to say "true" when he stopped himself.

What was he *doing?* It was time to admit his faults to his sister—and to himself. He was clever and did well in school, and he was a good pitcher, but he was far from perfect. He was hot-headed and, yes, arrogant. A friendly version of Hirth—but he had come to realize he had more of Hirth's cruel side than he ever realized. Instead of spending all his time telling others how great he was, maybe it was time to use his abilities to lift others up.

"I'm *not* great at everything, Jen. Not even close. I just keep at something until I master it. I figure, if there's an answer to be found, then why shouldn't I be able to find it. And I keep trying different things until I do. Sometimes I fall flat on my face, but mostly I succeed. Not because I'm just naturally talented at everything. But because I never give up."

Jenna shook her head in wonder. Everything he said made so much sense. "You're right. The only reason I was able to solve any of those riddles, or think of a question that would keep us from being executed on Mesrobia, was because I was confident and determined—and persistent."

"Exactly. You're finally catching on. That's my secret," said Zachary. "I don't get discouraged. I know that if I work at something hard enough I can do it. Raw talent alone won't get you very far. Not if you doubt yourself. Not if you aren't persistent and determined. But if you are, you can achieve great things—even *without* great ability. And here's the scary part, Jen. You can have it all! You're lucky enough to have the ability. Now, if you start believing in yourself, you're going to be unstoppable."

Jenna thought about all her recent experiences. He was so right. It was miraculous what a simple change in attitude could do for you.

"In fact," continued Zachary, "after what I've seen after we entered the first portal, my betting days with you are over. I'm too afraid of losing."

Jenna beamed. "Zachary. I never thought I'd be saying this, but— " She looked at him affectionately. "Thanks. Thanks for fooling me. I'm going to start believing in myself. I'll never give up on something again until I've given it all I have."

"In that case," said Zachary happily. "You'll probably be running the world before too long."

Jenna grinned. "Which one?" she said.

She had just been kidding around, but after Zachary returned her smile, her question caused both kids to suddenly remember where they were, and how unlikely it would be to ever see home again, and their brief good mood evaporated instantly.

Zachary sighed. "We'd better go check on Nivek," he said.

They journeyed to the section of the cave Nivek was in, calling out to let him know they were coming so he could turn away from them. They shielded the light from Jenna's shoe as they approached.

"How are your eyes?" asked Jenna, unable to help feeling guilty, even though Nivek had attacked them first.

"It took a while, but they gradually shook off the effect of your shoe-weapon, Jenna the Human. I'm good as new."

That was a relief. They talked for a few minutes longer and decided to hike through the cave in the hope of finding a portal. Jenna poured half of the Glow-leaves into her other shoe and gave it to her brother, allowing each of them to see several yards ahead. Nivek led the way, about ten feet in the lead, his back toward the humans and their light that, to him, was still blindingly bright. The lighting was much dimmer than the humans would have preferred and much brighter than Nivek would have preferred, but it was the only way they could walk together.

They hiked and talked for several hours, trading stories and becoming quite friendly. And then, from nowhere, not one but two portals appeared suddenly at their feet. Once again it seemed as though the portals were never too far away from them.

They looked through the first one—and saw nothing but blackness, even with both glowing shoes held over the portal. The second one revealed what looked like a tropical island.

They covered their glowing shoes and Nivek joined them to inspect the portals. He gasped beside them as he looked through the first one. "This is my home!" he said excitedly.

"You can *see* something through there?" asked Jenna. It had been pitch black.

"Oh yes. And I can tell the vegetation of my world immediately." He rubbed his head with the tip of a tentacle. "But I don't understand. How can this be here? The point I arrived at is about three miles away from here. I check it every day in the hope that the strange hole will return."

"Don't worry. It makes sense," said Zachary. "The strange holes—what we call portals—have their own logic. The incoming ones are usually different from the outgoing ones." Zachary paused. "But you'd better go through. You never know how long they'll stick around."

"I can't thank you both enough," said Nivek happily. "Sorry again for the, um . . . misunderstanding. Good luck finding your parents," he said.

They wished him well and then, without any ceremony, he took a small hop and was gone.

Jenna uncovered her shoe to once again reveal the many tiny Glow-leaves within. "Let's get out of here. I don't want to stay in this cave even a second longer."

Zachary smiled wearily. "I know what you mean."

They held hands, closed their eyes, and moved forward. Moments later they were standing on the tropical island they had seen through the portal. After several painful minutes their eyes adjusted to the daylight. Finally, they could see without holding a shoe in front of them.

For the first time in their lives, they appreciated the ability to see for the miracle that it was. Light had never been so dazzling. And *anywhere* was better than being in a dark cave.

And this was not just anywhere. This was a tropical paradise. The air was fresh and cool and everywhere they looked they could see beautiful, brightly colored tropical plants.

Jenna emptied her shoes of Glow-leaves and returned them to her feet. They began exploring the island. It was only a few miles across, but it was breathtaking. Along with the flowers and fruiting trees it was ringed by white-sand beaches. The ocean was unnaturally calm—as smooth as glass for as far as they could see. And instead of being blue, both it and the sky were a light shade of pink. But other than these differences—which were admittedly very strange—they could have been on a Pacific Island back home.

Zachary looked around. "Hey, we've been here several minutes and no one has tried to kill us yet," he said wryly.

"Yeah, the worlds have nothing in common except for being filled with dangerous beings who don't trust us," said Jenna miserably. "Not to mention wanting us dead."

Zachary considered. "It's not just that the worlds are dangerous," he said after a few seconds of thought. "It's how *quickly* the danger finds us. This has gotta be important. I mean, no one can be *that* unlucky."

Jenna raised her eyebrows. "Well, this island is as peaceful looking as it gets," she said hopefully. "Maybe our luck is finally changing."

Before her brother could respond a group of perhaps twenty natives suddenly emerged from behind a small grouping of trees.

"Of course, I could be wrong," muttered Jenna miserably as the natives surrounded them.

Their arms and legs were human-like, although much thicker and more muscled, but the rest of their bodies were lizard-like. Their skin was green and scaly and their teeth jutted out of both sides of their mouths in a roughly interlocking manner—like those of a crocodile. They each carried a long spear.

The tallest of the group came forward and faced Zachary, completely ignoring Jenna. "I am Fromm. Chief of the Wekla. What are you doing on our Island?" he demanded.

Zachary turned to Fromm and sighed heavily. Here we go again, he thought. "We're looking for our parents. We're not here to bother anyone. You haven't seen anyone who looks like us have you?"

"No. We haven't. But you can't just come here uninvited and look for them on *our* island. I'm afraid we can't let you continue until you have proven yourself worthy in battle. How tall are you?"

Zachary told him.

"Quist," he called out. A smaller native emerged from the group. "Quist here is your exact height. You will have to prove yourself by beating him in a fight. If you win you may proceed and we will leave you alone."

Zachary looked at Quist. He might have been Zachary's height but he was at least twice his weight, and probably four times his strength. Zachary didn't stand a chance against this Quist.

"But I don't have any reason to fight him," protested Zachary. "How about if we promise to leave your island as soon as we possibly can."

"Not good enough!" roared Fromm. "Are you a coward? You say you don't have a reason to fight. Let me give you one. Quist will be fighting you. Whether you choose to fight back or not is your business."

"How about letting us prove ourselves by answering riddles?" said Jenna hopefully.

"Absolutely not, Female!" spat Fromm as a look of disgust came over his face.

Jenna looked at her brother and shrugged her shoulders. "Worth a try," she said innocently.

Zachary fought back a smile.

Things were looking bad again, he thought. And it didn't appear that any clever ideas were going to save him from a beating. But after all of the lethal dangers they had narrowly dodged on the other worlds, he felt as though he was getting off easy this time. At least it was only a fight. At least he would survive.

"So who decides the winner?" he asked Fromm. It didn't really matter, he thought. It wasn't as if he had a chance anyway.

"Don't worry," said Fromm. "That will be easy." The chief of the lizard-men smiled broadly. "Because the fight will be to the death."

CHAPTER TWENTY-FOUR

Circles

The pattern was repeating again, thought Jenna. As always, they were now in a fight for their lives within a short time after entering a new world.

But were both of their lives in danger or just Zachary's? He was being forced to fight Quist but the tribe appeared to be ignoring her. They didn't seem to think very highly of females. She sensed she needed to explore this further. "Then after my brother fights, will I have to?" she asked.

The entire group of natives roared in laughter. "You?" said Fromm in disbelief. "You're nothing but a female. We are a brave and noble people. Of course we won't fight you. You are free to go at any time."

Jenna nodded. Just as she had thought. *Nothing but a female, huh?* Well, she would see about that. If they wanted to ignore her, so much the better. She would find a way to make them regret it. Since they were harassing her brother, it would be up to her to come up with a plan to get them out of this.

Jenna concentrated so hard that she barely heard her brother as he asked about the rules and tried desperately to stall for time. There must be a way to outwit these annoying beings.

But how? Once again, she needed to find a way to use their own traits against them. They obviously thought they were tough and courageous, and far superior to a mere female. How could she use this knowledge to goad them into doing something stupid?

She continued thinking while her brother tried, unsuccessfully, to talk his way out of the contest. Fromm was quickly losing patience with him. He was seconds away from ordering the fight to begin.

And then, from out of nowhere, she remembered a trick that a classmate had played on her several years earlier. It was one of only a few times she had been fooled by someone other than Zachary. A modified version of this trick would be just the thing to use.

But she had to play it just right.

"Hold on, Quist!" she said boldly, just as Fromm was about to begin the fight. "It's obvious that you can beat my scrawny brother in a fight. What will that prove? Only that you're the biggest coward that anyone has ever seen," she taunted.

"No one calls me a coward!" roared Quist in fury. "I don't care if you are a female. If you say that again, you'll regret it."

"Yeah, yeah, yeah," said Jenna, unimpressed. "Big words. We both know you can easily kill me. For that matter, we both know that you can easily kill my brother. But before you bore yourself with that, I was wondering if you wanted to find out just how tough you really are."

What are you doing? mouthed Zachary. *Are you out of your mind?*

Trust me, she mouthed back quickly.

Even through his rage, Quist knew he had to at least listen to what Jenna had to say or risk looking as though he had backed down in front of his tribe. "What are you talking about?" he snapped.

"I propose a different contest. One that will be a real challenge for you," continued Jenna. "One that I'm sure will be *too much* of a challenge for you." She paused. "Would you say that you're about three times my weight?"

Quist smirked. "At least, Female," he said with contempt.

"Well I think that you're such a spineless coward that I can force you to move from the spot you're standing on. *Me*—several inches shorter than you and a third of your weight." Jenna sneered at him. "Not to mention a female." She raised her eyebrows. "You're not afraid of a female, are you?"

"Of course not," responded Quist immediately.

Jenna leaned closer to him. She knew that one would get him. "You will be," she whispered menacingly. "And you won't be able to stand your ground either. I can get you to move. I don't think you're tough. I think you're a huge chicken."

"A what?"

Whoops, she thought. Apparently they didn't know about chickens. "A big coward," she amended. "And I can prove it by getting you to move."

"No way," said Quist. "A female? Impossible! You're out of your mind."

"Am I?" responded Jenna. "Let's find out. I'll tell you what. You stand there and I'll walk in circles around you. Three circles. I'll circle you once, then I'll circle you twice. And I'm so sure that you're nothing but a weak little coward, that by the time I circle you the third time you'll have moved from where you're standing. Are you brave enough for the challenge?"

"I'm brave enough for anything you could possibly throw at me, *Female*," Quist growled hatefully. "I'll do it. Nothing you can do could ever get me to move. And after I've shown you that you're crazy, I'll make your brother suffer even more to pay for your insults."

"Fine," said Jenna. "But what if you do move?"

"What do you mean?" asked Quist.

"What if I'm right, and you're so gutless that I get you to move from the spot before I finish circling you the third time?"

Quist shook his head. "It doesn't matter. It won't happen."

"If it does, do you agree to let us stay on your island as long as we need to and not harm us?"

Quist looked over to Fromm who, along with Zachary and the rest of the gathering, had been listening, spellbound, to the entire exchange.

Fromm nodded.

"Okay," said Quist. "I agree."

"Do all of you agree?" she said to the rest of the group.

They all nodded their agreement.

"Okay. Even though I will prove Quist a coward, I'm counting on him and your people to be men of your word."

"You have nothing to worry about," snapped Fromm. "We would die before breaking our word. If you do what you claim you will have full run of the island."

"I will accept your puny challenge, of course," said Quist. "But I smell a trick. For instance, how far do you have to get me to move? Everybody moves a little. You can't claim victory just because I moved a few inches accidentally."

"Three feet," said Jenna with confidence.

"Three feet?" repeated Quist. "You really are crazy. You think you can get me to move three feet just by circling me? How are you going to measure?"

"No measurement. It will be obvious that you've moved *at least* three feet," answered Jenna.

"Okay. But if you attack me, I will defend myself," he said.

"Don't worry, *coward*. I'm not going to attack you. I won't need to. A frightened little boy like you will move on your own."

It was obvious that Jenna's repeated barbs were driving Quist mad. If it were not for the presence of Fromm he would have torn Jenna's head from her shoulders by now.

"Do your best to frighten me, Female!" Quist snarled. "Come on. Get me to move from this spot."

He bared a mouthful of sharp, pointy teeth, and glared at her hatefully. "And when this nonsense is over and you have failed miserably—I want you to stick around to see what I'm going to do to your brother."

CHAPTER TWENTY-FIVE

The Realization

Jenna smiled. She had him.

She dug her heel in the ground to mark the beginning of the circle and began walking slowly around Quist. He spun so that he was always facing her as she did so. When she came back to the mark she had made in the ground she looked at the group and said, "One."

The crowd looked on expectantly. She had not attacked Quist or made any hostile move to frighten him. He was still firmly planted on the spot he had been on. Zachary watched her worriedly, hoping she knew what she was doing.

Jenna began circling Quist again. "Two," she said calmly as she completed the circle.

And then she stopped.

She looked at Quist and grinned broadly. Then, shrugging her shoulders innocently, she began walking away from him.

"Where are you going, Female?" Quist yelled after her.

She turned around to face him again. "To the other end of the island, of course. I can't stay here all day."

"Hah," said Quist triumphantly. "You're giving up."

"Not at all," said Jenna happily. "I said that I would circle you once, then circle you again. And that you would move before I finished circling you for the third time. Stay there. Maybe I'll decide to come back in a few years and finish the third circle."

Quist just stared at her stupidly, but the truth slowly dawned on Fromm, who glowered angrily. They had all been tricked. He was not pleased. This clever female had made fools of them. But he had made an agreement with her. "You win. You two are free to roam the island," he spat.

"But I haven't moved yet," said Quist.

"Fool!" barked Fromm angrily. "She tricked you. She said you would move before she completed her third circle. Well, she obviously has no intention of *ever* completing it. The only way for you to win is to stay within three feet of where you are now until you die. If you're willing to stand there like an idiot until you drop dead, you're welcome to do so."

Fromm led the group back the way they had come, not even giving Jenna or Zachary a backward glance. When they were almost out of sight of Quist who was still rooted to his original spot, Fromm turned back toward him. "Well, are you coming? It wasn't just you she fooled. None of us saw this coming. This will not be a black mark against your bravery or honor."

Quist shot a hateful look at Jenna and then scampered off after the rest of the group.

Zachary grinned and ran over to join his sister. "Where did you learn how to be such a master scam artist?" he said in admiration.

"I learned the hard way," she replied. "By being the victim of your scams so often."

Zachary laughed. "Well you've got it down perfectly. If scamming were karate you'd be a double black belt."

She had done a masterful job of getting underneath Quist's skin—or his scales at any rate—enraging and distracting him and making him so desperate to prove his bravery that he was certain to accept her challenge. "Congratulations," he added.

Jenna smiled. "Thanks. That means a lot coming from the master of scams."

"And thanks for getting me out of that," he added earnestly.

"You're very welcome," she said. "You know what this means, don't you," she added with a crooked smile. "It means that you were right. You remember our conversation back home during dinner before this whole crazy journey began?"

Zachary thought back. It seemed like hundreds of years had passed since then. He nodded.

"You were saying that our sparring—I think that was the word Mom used—that our sparring actually could help us. Well, your conning me certainly did. If you hadn't tricked me so many times so I knew how it was done, we'd have never gotten past those lizard-men."

Zachary looked guilty. "Well . . . yeah," he said. "I guess so. But really the only way it should have helped you is learning how *not* to be tricked—not how to trick others. To be fair, Mom and Dad were right also. I mean, it came in handy here, but tricking people isn't exactly the most important skill you could learn."

Jenna laughed. "I guess you're right. Not unless you want to be a used-car salesman."

Zachary smiled. "Or a con-artist."

"Or a carnival pitchman."

Zachary was about to continue when he felt an odd sensation in his brain. He had been certain that he didn't have enough pieces of the puzzle to figure out what was happening to them, or their parents. But suddenly he wasn't so sure. For some strange reason there was something about the conversation they had had in their kitchen, just floating out of reach, that could help pull everything together.

He concentrated for all he was worth. What was it? What was the clue he needed?

He couldn't find it. It was like having an itch in his brain that he couldn't scratch.

Jenna sighed. "I keep telling myself not to think about home," she said wistfully. "But I keep doing it anyway. I would give anything to have things back to normal. To sit at the kitchen table and eat one of Mom's terrible meals. To lose bets to you—even if I have to do your chores. And especially to listen to Mom and Dad tease you about growing up to be a used-car salesman."

"Me too," said Zachary wearily.

He paused and then cleared his throat. "About that bet," he began. "After everything we've been through—not to mention that you keep saving my life—if we ever do get back, I release you from having to do my chores."

"Really?"

"Absolutely."

This news didn't really raise her spirits, but she tried to fake it a little for Zachary's benefit. "Great," she said flatly, unable to manage any enthusiasm. "Then what are we waiting for? Let's find Mom and Dad and get home."

Zachary nodded. He tried to force a smile, but failed. The danger just kept coming. And there was very little sign that they were making any progress in learning what was going on, or had any chance of finding their parents.

But once again, he had a strange feeling that the answer was very close, although at the moment, just beyond his reach. What was the clue? He strained. He willed it to come closer. He could almost reach out and touch it.

"Zack," said Jenna excitedly, interrupting his thoughts. "Look."

There was the familiar shimmer of a portal directly in front of them.

They walked over to it and looked down. And they saw . . . nothing.

"Just great," complained Jenna. They had seen an arctic world, a desert world, and a cave world. To what type of world would this portal lead them? They could be in for quite a nasty surprise.

"We might as well take it," said Zachary unhappily. "What else are we going to do? Staying on this island won't help us. We already know that Mom and Dad weren't here."

Jenna reluctantly agreed.

They held hands and closed their eyes. "One, two, three," they yelled as they jumped through.

They opened their eyes. *What now?*

They were on a gently sloping plateau, high up in a magnificent mountain range. The mountains were covered by a blanket of short grass; grass that covered every inch of every mountain and looked to be at the exact same height everywhere. A green on a golf course couldn't have been more uniform.

A few tall, skinny trees dotted the landscape around them. The trees each had six giant leaves, thirty or so feet above the ground, that were smooth and unbroken, as if they were made of plastic. The leaves were deep blue in color and were enormous. At least six feet long and three feet wide. Far down below, at the base of the mountain, was a thick woods.

Given that they hadn't been able to see through the portal, they had been lucky. They could have landed somewhere far worse.

"I guess we should head to the bottom," suggested Zachary. "Ahhhhh," he yelled as he tried to take the first step and slipped, sliding for about ten feet before he could stop himself. "Be careful," he warned. "This grass is really slippery."

Jenna nodded and carefully joined him. When she reached him he was staring into the sky like a zombie. She followed his line of sight. A giant, prehistoric looking bird-thing was flying menacingly through the air hundreds of yards away. It was scaly like a lizard and as long as a bus, with the wingspan of a small plane. It had wicked talons large enough to easily grip a grown man.

"Now I know what a worm must feel like when it sees a bird," said Jenna, as the prehistoric flying reptile flew out of site over the horizon. "If one of those things flies in this direction, we're in big trouble."

Zachary ignored her. His head was tilted back and he was deep in thought.

Jenna surveyed the area once more. "I think I know what we need to do. We need to get to the base of this mountain and into the woods. Those Pterodactyl-things can't fly in the woods, so we'll be safe. The grass is as slippery as snow and grows all the way to the bottom. So if we can think of a way to get one of those huge leaves from the tree over there, we can use it as a sled."

Zachary didn't even hear her. The answer to everything they had been through was finally coming into focus. He strained with all of his might.

Bingo.

Finally—*finally.* The puzzle clicked into place in Zachary's mind.

He had an answer. It had to be right. It was the only answer that could possibly explain everything that had happened to them.

Zachary finally broke out of his trance. He turned to his sister, his eyes wide. "Jenna, he said. "I've finally figured it out."

"Figured *what* out?" said Jenna.

Zachary stared at her intently. "Everything," he said simply.

CHAPTER TWENTY-SIX

The Solution

"The portals, the dangers . . . all of this," said Zachary. "None of it is real. We're just pawns in a chess game. The subjects of some kind of experiment."

Jenna's forehead wrinkled in confusion. "An experiment?" she repeated.

Zachary nodded. "Just before we left the island I had a feeling I was getting close to a solution. When we were talking about the night we left home. About my scams and how Mom and Dad teased me at dinner. Teased me about becoming a used-car salesman, or a con-man, or a carnival pitchman. But there was one more item on that list. Do you remember what else they said I might be good at?"

Jenna tried to replay the conversation in her mind. "They said you would also make a good lab rat," she whispered.

"Exactly. *A lab rat*. Part of my mind knew something about that conversation was important. And when I remembered the lab rat part, I knew that this was the answer. Someone is putting us through a maze—testing us. We're lab rats in someone's experiment. What we're going through just isn't possible in the *real* universe. We've talked about how incredibly bad our luck has been. How deadly dangers find us almost immediately after we come to each new world. Every single time." He shook his head. "It's impossible for anyone to be *that* unlucky."

"In case you haven't noticed, it's also impossible to go through a portal in our kitchen and end up on other worlds. You can't jump to the conclusion this is some kind of test just based on that."

"Yes I can. Because *luck* has nothing to do with any of this. We've been forced to face these dangers *on purpose*. But if you think about it, even though the dangers keep coming, we always have the chance to figure out a way to survive them. I mean, if we landed on a planet the size of Jupiter we'd be dead instantly. Or if the Mesrobians had just killed us on sight, there'd be nothing we could've done about it. But in each case there was a single way out—and we were being tested to see if we could find it."

Jenna thought about what he said for several long seconds, but still wasn't convinced.

"On Orum," continued Zachary, "what are the chances the ping-pong ball would fall into that little hole? What are the chances that a hole would even be there? One in a million? One in a *billion*? We were being tested. You didn't fumble the ping-pong ball. The testers caused it to fall and roll into the hole. And they chose to use ping-pong balls for a good reason: because we know they float. And there just happened to be a well nearby filled with water. Leaving us with one way out, if we could pass the test and find it."

Jenna considered. He did have a point. The ridiculously low overpass that was impossible for their car to pass through, unless they deflated the tires, was like this as well. And they had saved Tular within minutes of reaching his world. If they hadn't had an expert helping them, they wouldn't have lasted ten minutes there. A Harpoon Tulip or Swordbird or something else would have killed them.

The only way Tular would have trusted them enough to help them is if they saved his life. It did make a strange kind of sense if they were being tested. To pass they had to choose to save Tular and find a way to do it. She mentioned this to her brother.

Zachary nodded. "And the Grull were so rare that Tular had never seen one before. What are the chances that he would be attacked by one right when we were about to go through the portal? Thinking back, it's as if someone wanted to see what we would do. Would we go through? Or would we create a diversion so we could save Tular and his clan?"

"And even beyond that," added Jenna, "would *you* go through and leave your sister behind? Or would you stay with her to face the deadly and horrible Grull?" Jenna shook her head. "If you *are* right, someone sure knows how to make a tough test, that's for sure."

Jenna paused in thought for several seconds, and realized there was a major flaw in her brother's reasoning. "But then what's with Mom and Dad? Why did they disappear? And why did they insist we not come after them?"

"I think the bird's message was a fake," said Zachary. "I mean, how did the bird possibly find us, anyway? I think it was just the first part of the test. The bird's message made it clear that Mom and Dad were in big trouble. And the testers made sure we knew that time was racing by for them, so we would realize we couldn't wait for outside help. The experimenters wanted to see if we would disobey our parents and risk our lives to try to save them, not knowing what we would be facing; only that it would be incredibly dangerous."

"If that's true, then I probably didn't really see Mom and Dad in the cave, either," noted Jenna.

It had been odd that the portal had been two-way for sight, but only one-way for sound. She could hear her parents, but they couldn't hear her, or answer any of her questions. And why did they insist she jump through to *them*? Not knowing where Zachary was, they would never have abandoned him. They would have insisted on jumping through to her.

Zachary nodded. "I think Mom and Dad's appearance in the cave—or *supposed* appearance—was just another test. The experimenters were tempting you. They wanted to see what you would do. Would you jump into the arms of your parents? Or would you stay trapped in a cave, blind and helpless, and try to save your brother from a tentacled monster? Knowing that you had almost no chance."

"So you think some tester in a lab-coat was just watching us the whole time as we moved from world to world. Taking notes."

"Right," agreed Zachary. "Using Mom and Dad as the lure to keep us moving."

They remained silent for several long seconds, lost in thought.

"But why?" said Jenna. "And *who*?"

Zachary blew out a long breath. "Hirth and Wyland, that's who. Our see-through friends from Orum. I'm almost certain."

"Based on what?" asked Jenna.

"Remember just before we drove off and left them, Hirth said we would never find Mom and Dad. I told him we would. Do you remember what he said then?"

Jenna searched her memory. "Something about us being stupid and not having any chance."

Zachary shook his head. "No. I remember it exactly. He said we would 'flunk miserably.' He used the word 'flunk' Jenna. Remember, he and Wyland were very precise with their words. He could have said 'fail' but he said 'flunk'. And flunk is a word you only use when talking about a test."

"I don't know Zack. You've decided they're behind this based on a single *word*? Maybe you're just not remembering right."

"I'm remembering right," he insisted. "But there's more. I didn't tell you about it because I thought I'd imagined it." He paused. "Right before you rescued me in the cave, I took out the language transformer Hirth had given me, and tried my hardest to see it. I couldn't. But for just a second, I could see *myself*, and Nivek, from *above*. Clear as day. And not with my eyes, but with my *mind*."

Jenna's face wrinkled up in confusion. "I don't get it?"

Zachary was about to respond when one of the giant, leathery-winged prehistoric monsters swooped down out of nowhere. It flew toward them with alarming speed.

"Split up!" yelled Zachary as he moved away from his sister, making the creature choose between targets.

The monster swooped down toward Zachary, its powerful talons extended. Zachary dived to the ground and flattened out, causing the creature to miss him by inches.

The creature flew off hundreds of yards distant and began making a huge, lazy circle to come around for another attempt. It had sized them up and knew that it had all the time in the world. They were slow and completely out in the open. Easy prey.

Zachary stood to his full height. "Jenna, I need to finish," he said hurriedly. "What I saw in the cave—I've figured out what it means. That crystal Hirth gave us isn't just a language transformer. It's also a sort of spy camera. Somehow, Hirth and Wyland are using it to keep track of us. If you're going to run rats through a maze, you have to have some way to watch them. Somehow, I was able to tap into it in the cave. For just an instant. I thought I'd imagined it, but when I figured out the rest, it suddenly made perfect sense."

Jenna had barely listened to him, having rushed over to one of the trees with the giant, plastic-looking leaves. "Zack!" she screamed. "Come on. We need to figure out how to get one of these leaves so we can sled down the mountain and hide from this thing. *Come on!*"

Zachary shook his head. "Forget about escape, Jenna," he said. "We're not running anymore."

The flying creature had completed its turn and was now bearing down on them at an ever increasing speed.

"Come on, Zack!" pleaded Jenna in horror as the creature extended its deadly talons.

"No. It's nothing but a test. I refuse to run the maze anymore."

"But what if you're wrong!" screamed Jenna. "*You can't bet your life on this.*"

"I can!" said Zachary, his eyes fiery. "And I am!"

Zachary threw back his head. "I refuse to play along anymore!" he screamed to the sky at the top of his lungs. "Hirth and Wyland, and whoever else might be behind this, I'm done playing. Get yourself another guinea pig!" he finished angrily. "I'm not moving!"

He glared defiantly at the giant, flying reptile bearing down upon him. Its mighty talons were fully extended and it was only seconds away.

"*Zack, dive!*" screamed Jenna hysterically.

Zachary didn't move.

The giant beast altered its course at the very last instant, its talons so close they raked the very top layer of Zachary's hair. It then retracted its talons and rose in the sky, flying away.

Jenna's mouth fell open. *He had been right.* About *everything.*

Zachary pulled the purple crystal from his pocket and held it in front of his face. "Now how about telling us what this is all about," he growled.

Zachary waited patiently for a response while Jenna walked over to join him. The moment she was at his side, Wyland's voice was broadcast from the crystal as if it were a speaker. "Well done, humans," he said. "Wait where you are. We'll be there to escort you through a portal to Orum in just a few minutes." There was a pause. "And then you will get the answers that you seek."

CHAPTER TWENTY-SEVEN

The Explanation

Hirth and Wyland joined them about five minutes later, as promised. The difference in expressions between the two transparent men was even greater than before. Hirth looked more bitter and angry than ever, while Wyland looked delighted. Both men asked that conversation be delayed until they were back on their world.

Less than ten minutes after they had joined Jenna and Zachary, the two transparent men had escorted them to a nearby portal. They stepped through and were once again on Orum, with its familiar rolling hills and farmhouses.

"Congratulations to you both," began Wyland as soon as they arrived. "You were, indeed, engaged in a test. One you passed with flying colors."

"*That remains to be seen*," challenged Hirth.

Wyland glared at Hirth and said, "I let you be in charge when they first arrived, and you agreed to let me be in charge for this part. I know this was easy for you to agree to, since you never believed they would live long enough to even leave Orum. Especially after you infected them with Anchor Fungus, a clear violation of our agreement. But they *did* survive: your Anchor Fungus and far more.

Hirth folded his arms but did not reply.

"Please ignore him," said Wyland to the two humans.

"What have you done with our parents?" demanded Zachary. Wyland may have been friendlier than Hirth, but Zachary had no reason to trust him.

"Don't worry," said Wyland. "Yes we um . . . borrowed . . . them temporarily, but they've been treated like royalty. We'll take you to them very soon."

Jenna and Zachary glanced at each other and blew out long breaths of relief. *Their parents were alive and well*. And they would—finally—be reunited with them. Both kids felt as if a crushing weight had just been lifted from their chests.

Jenna turned back toward Wyland. "What is this all about?" she asked.

"Our two worlds are about to become linked," said Wyland. "Extensively linked."

"How?" said Zachary. "And what do you mean by *extensively*?"

"Let me begin at the beginning," said Wyland. "Portals link together numerous worlds as you've seen. Thousands and thousands of them, in fact. But they are a natural

239

phenomenon. No one can create or control them. They appear for unknown reasons at unknown places." He paused. "A few months ago, we became aware that a single portal had opened between us and a new world." He nodded at the two humans. "*Your* world. With thousands more in the process of becoming born."

Zachary's eyes widened. "Thousands?" he repeated. He scratched his head. "Do all of them link our two worlds, or do some go to other worlds?"

"Very insightful question, Zachary. Inexplicably, every last one of them links only our two worlds, Orum and Earth. Or they will when they are fully born in just a few weeks time." He paused. "Until this one active portal opened, fairly recently, your planet Earth was completely isolated from all other planets."

"Will any of them be two-way portals?" asked Jenna.

"As far as we can tell," said Wyland, "they will *all* be two-way. To our knowledge, Orum and Earth will be connected more extensively than any two worlds have ever been."

Whoa, thought Zachary. Incredible.

"Anyway," continued Wyland. "Given how closely our worlds are about to be linked, we decided to bring sixty adult humans to Orum to study."

Zachary nodded knowingly. "A bit nervous about the new neighbors, huh?" he said. He couldn't really blame them. If he could choose where the Earth portals led, he doubted if it would be here. Surely there were species that were more compatible with humans than these transparent people.

This time Wyland's smile was forced. "Let's just say we wanted to understand your species a little better. After all, we have portals on our planet to any number of worlds, but no more than three, maximum, to any single world."

"And you're about to have thousands linking you and Earth," said Jenna.

"Exactly."

"Not a good situation, is it?" said Zachary. "Because other than Orum, Earth will still be isolated. For humans to get to any other worlds, they'll have to go through yours."

"The thought had occurred to us," said Wyland grimly.

The alien paused to let Jenna and Zachary digest what he had said so far, and then continued. "In discussions with the humans we brought here, we found that you have no concept of magic. Other than in your stories for children. But not real magic. And when we demonstrated magic, it made the subjects we brought here uncomfortable. For civilizations of your level of sophistication, inability to do even the smallest feat of magic is unheard of.

"We also took humans to numerous other worlds, including insect worlds," continued Wyland, "to see how they would react." He shook his head. "And they did *not* handle it well. They were often unable to adjust to new situations—probably because Earth has always been isolated and never exposed to any alien creatures or cultures. But based on this we were concerned that if Earth were brought into contact with our world, and through us to endless others, this could lead to disaster. Your species is too unimaginative and close-minded to be able to embrace beings and concepts vastly different from yourselves. You're too inflexible. Too unprepared to accept what you believe to be impossible."

"So were our parents part of this group you're talking about?" asked Jenna.

Wyland shook his head. "No. They were others of your kind. We used magic to erase their memories and returned them home." He paused. "And then our Grand Council deliberated."

"Grand Council?" said Zachary, raising his eyebrows.

"The ruling body of our world. A collection of the twenty most powerful wielders of magic on Orum. What you might call witches and wizards. Although we prefer the term *magicians*. But unlike those who call themselves magicians on your planet, who only *pretend* to do magic, we use real magic in everyday life. Each member of the Grand Council is the most powerful magician on Orum in their specialty area."

"Um . . . okay," said Jenna. "So what did your Grand Council have to say about the situation?"

Wyland lowered his eyes. "We took a vote. Under the circumstances, the Council decided it would be best to keep Earth isolated. Forever. To destroy your portals."

"I thought you couldn't do that," said Zachary.

"We can't create them or control them. But we can definitely destroy them or stop them as they're about to emerge. Anyway," he continued, "I had studied Earth and disagreed with this course of action. I thought we had a lot to learn from your people."

"*Really?*" said Zachary wryly. "From a non-magic species like ours? What did you think you could learn?"

"Teamwork, for one," replied Wyland. "Our species never needed it. When you're able to use magic fairly effortlessly, there isn't much need to cooperate. Since your people couldn't use magic, you often needed teamwork to survive, especially during your primitive phase. So you're a species who have evolved to work in a pack, while we're like your cats: not great at working together. Not very cooperative."

Both kids glanced at Hirth, his arms still folded on his chest as he radiated hostility, and decided he and Wyland offered a great example of an inability to work together. But two humans who hated each other would act the same way, so this didn't necessarily prove anything.

"The other skill I thought we could learn from your species is logic and problem-solving," continued Wyland. "When you can use magic, you don't need to understand *why* things work the way they do. But your species has always had a handicap. Because you've never been able to use magic, you were forced to learn to solve problems the *hard* way." He paused. "I argued to the Grand Council that it would be a mistake to cut off our worlds from each other. I also sensed that your species was becoming more open minded. More accepting. I was convinced that the next generation," he gestured toward Jenna and Zachary. "*Your* generation, would be able to handle surprises far better than the current one."

"So you proposed a test?" said Zachary.

Wyland nodded. "Exactly. A test of the potential of the human species. The potential of the next generation. I proposed we select two children and test their flexibility. Their reaction to the unexpected. Their ability to fight irrational instincts. Like an aversion to giant wasps, for instance. Their ability to tolerate, accept, and even embrace differences. Different concepts, different cultures, different beings. Their ability to change perspective. To accept new ideas. It would be a truly brutal test. Under the most difficult conditions. With their lives always on the line. If they passed, I got the Grand Council to agree not to close the portals between our worlds."

He paused to catch his breath and then continued. "And I wanted it to be more than a test. I wanted my people to have a chance to study humans in action. To study their teamwork, and their problem solving. To see how much we might be able to learn from your species."

"How did we do?" said Jenna.

"As I told you already," said Wyland, beaming, "you passed brilliantly. You surpassed even my high expectations. You accepted and befriended others no matter how troubling their appearance was to you. You were able to see beyond their appearances and judge them by what was on the inside. Your teamwork was extraordinary, and the Grand Council got to see all that I hoped we could learn from you. You stuck by each other no matter what. You made sacrifices for each other. And the bleaker things got, the more you supported each other. You demonstrated generosity. Compassion. Self-sacrifice. Bravery. Determination. Loyalty. Resourcefulness. Adaptability." Wyland paused. "I could go on, but I think you get the point."

"Thanks," said both kids at once, delighted by the compliments but still wary of the situation they found themselves in. There were still a lot of unanswered questions.

"And then, *unbelievably*," continued Wyland, "you managed to figure out you were being tested. Truly remarkable!" he gushed.

Iirth snorted, the first time he had been anything but a statue for some time. "If you hadn't made sure they knew there was an answer to find before they left," he snapped, "they would never have guessed they were being tested."

"I'm having trouble remembering," said Wyland. "Can you help me? Which of us was the idiot who used the word *flunk*?"

A look of pure hatred came over Hirth's face.

"So was none of what happened real, then?" asked Zachary.

"Oh no," replied Wyland. "It was all very, very real. We had teams of magicians from Orum working invisibly in the background to ensure you got into the proper . . . trouble. Lesser magicians than those on the Grand Council, but still quite powerful. But you really did help Lisgar get home to her family. She would not have done so without you. And you helped Nivek get back to his world as well. And you saved Tular's life. And so on."

Zachary tilted his head in thought. "And you made sure that all of the worlds we visited had fairly primitive societies—without magic."

Wyland beamed. "Exactly," he said. He turned to Hirth. "Even you have to see how well they're able to use reason to work things out. The problem solving abilities of *our* people are growing weaker with every generation, but the minds of these humans are working out puzzles all the time, not just when they're solving riddles on Mesrobia."

Wyland turned back to Zachary. "Most societies are able to perform magic to some degree, even when they're primitive. But there are a very rare few that don't develop this ability until their societies mature. We made sure to limit your travels to these worlds." He paused. "But there is only one world we know of that has an advanced society, but a total inability to perform even the smallest feat of magic."

"Earth?" said Jenna.

"I'm afraid so," replied Wyland.

"So speaking of Earth," said Jenna. "Of all the people on our planet, why did you choose *us* for this test?"

"I'm a master in all areas of magic," said Wyland proudly. "But I'm a grandmaster, the best on Orum, in magical intuition."

"Isn't intuition when you kind of know something," said Jenna, "but you aren't sure *how* you know it?"

"Exactly. I often don't have this power, especially when it comes to my own future, but when I do, I'm never wrong. As part of this talent, I can sense the potential in people better than anyone else. Qualities both hidden and obvious. If you ask me to find the greatest singer in the world, I can do so. They may never have had a singing lesson in their lives, but I can tell without hearing them once that they can go on to perform brilliantly. Of all the children on Earth, my magic told me that you two had the best chance of passing this test. I don't know why this is—I just know that it *is*." He raised his eyebrows. "This didn't mean that you *would* pass, by the way, just that you would have the best chance of anyone. The odds were still very much against you."

Jenna couldn't help but feel outraged. "I appreciate that you didn't want Earth to be, um . . . isolated," she said angrily. "But the odds are that we would be killed! Didn't that matter to you? You were willing to see two innocent kids be killed just to prove a point to your Grand Council?"

"It sounds bad, I know," admitted Wyland. "But this was the only proposal the Grand Council would accept. And the alternative was shutting down the portals." He raised his eyebrows. "And since the Grand Council estimated this would cost over twenty million human lives, I thought risking yours was worth it."

Both kids stared at Wyland in horror. *Twenty million lives?*

"What are you talking about?" demanded Zachary. "Why would shutting down the portals hurt anyone?"

"We've learned that your portals have been emerging for many of your generations. Along a very long jagged line that goes on for about eight hundred miles, in a place you call California. As the portals get closer to emergence, they have been known to cause what you call *earthquakes.*"

Zachary suddenly had a sick feeling in the pit of his stomach. "This jagged line. Is this what we call the San Andreas Fault?" he asked.

"I don't know what you call it. But I'm sure it isn't a geologic feature you could possibly fail to notice. You just didn't know this line was due to the birthing pains of thousands of portals."

"So what happens when you shut the portals down?" whispered Jenna, bracing herself for an answer she knew she wouldn't like.

"If the portals are allowed to emerge, they will stabilize the entire region. But if we destroy them all, this would have the opposite effect. Basically, much of the place you call California would be destroyed with them. This region would break apart into thousands of pieces, or perhaps even fall into your ocean."

Zachary felt dizzy. They had been fighting for their own lives, and the lives of their parents, completely unaware of how many *other* lives were in the balance. He couldn't remember exactly, but he was sure well over thirty million people lived in California. So the Grand Council may have even *underestimated* the number of deaths.

Wyland smiled. "Cheer up," he said warmly. "I know this is a horrifying thought to you. But now it's not going to happen. You've passed the test. Because of you, the portals will be allowed to open and stabilize this eight hundred mile stretch of land. Now you have nothing to worry about."

"*Guess again!*" hissed Hirth.

No one had paid attention to him for some time, but his words caused the two humans and Wyland to turn toward him instantly, just in time to see him rise five feet in the air, glowing from head to toe.

Zachary gulped. Maybe there was something to this magic thing, after all.

A diamond-shaped green crystal floated near his forehead, sparkling with the dazzling light of a thousand stars.

Wyland gasped and caused an orange crystal to shoot from his pocket and begin to position itself in front of him, but it was too late. An invisible force lanced out from Hirth's crystal and stabbed at the transparent man and the two siblings.

And all three fell to the ground, completely paralyzed from the neck down.

Then a second bolt of pure force emerged from the crystal, driving the three paralyzed victims into unconsciousness.

CHAPTER TWENTY-EIGHT

Trapped

Zachary opened his eyes groggily and realized in relief that he was no longer paralyzed. He looked around. He was in a woods, although one that was very thin, containing numerous large trees, but each was spaced much farther apart than in any woods back home. Large boulders appeared frequently in open spaces and smooth stones were strewn about like leaves after a storm. There was an eerie green cast to the sky. Was he still even on Orum?

He heard a noise to his left and yanked his head around to see what had caused it. It was Jenna! Alive and well.

But standing beside her was . . . he didn't know.

It was an alien. About three feet tall and wearing a long, shimmering blue robe that contained at least ten pockets. The being had a thick torso, flat face, and huge, glassy black eyes. It's ears were more on top of its head than on the sides. It wasn't an exact match, but if it had fur, it could well have been a close cousin of an *Ewok*.

"Glad to see you're awake," said the alien. "We've been awake for a few minutes now."

Zachary gasped. Its voice was Wyland's. What was going on *now*?

"Hirth's actions took me completely off guard," continued the short alien. "So I couldn't put up any resistance." He lowered his head. "For that, I am truly sorry."

"Wyland?" croaked Zachary.

The furless Ewok nodded.

"What happened?" he said in alarm. "Did Hirth turn you into a . . ." Zachary held out his hands helplessly. "Into a short, squat, man-thing?" he finished.

Wyland shook his head. "No. This is my true form," he said, ignoring Zachary's less than complimentary description of him. "And what you see around you is the true nature of Orum."

"I don't understand," said Zachary.

"Neither did Jenna," said Wyland. "But I wanted to wait until you were awake, so I could explain to both of you at the same time." Wyland took a deep breath. "Of all the wizards on Orum," he began, "Hirth is the most powerful. He is skilled in all areas of magic, but his specialty is illusion, for which he stands unequaled. He can make lesser magicians, and especially non-magicians, see whatever he wants them to see."

Both kids still looked confused.

"The Grand Council decided that while we were studying humans, and also for your test, it would be better if you didn't see us as we really are. The transparent beings you've seen here—including the hog," he added, "were just hallucinations. Illusions generated by Hirth. As were the hills, farmhouses, and sky. You didn't think something as bizarre as people who are totally see-through could actually exist, did you?"

Zachary frowned. It did seem unlikely "But why?" he asked.

"For many reasons. To throw humans off in case any of you managed to escape and return to your world. And with respect to you, so we could observe, during the first minutes of your test, how you reacted to beings we knew would be repulsive to you. To keep you off balance. And because the form of a hulking transparent man might seem more threatening to you than our real form."

Zachary grinned. "You think?"

Jenna couldn't help but laugh out loud. "Yeah. No offense, Wyland, but not only don't you look threatening, you kind of look, well . . . adorable. It's probably the big black eyes," she added, the grin still on her face.

"I've been noticing you're not speaking the way you did when we first arrived, either," said Zachary. "Everything isn't literal. Earlier, you said we passed the test with *flying colors*, for example. When we first spoke to you, if we had used this phrase, you'd have said something like, 'we're not flying, and what do colors have to do with a test?'"

Wyland beamed in delight. "You don't miss much, do you? You are correct. I convinced the Council that we should greet you the way we did, and use the speech patterns that we did, to further throw you off balance."

"But that wasn't the real reason, was it?" guessed Jenna.

"You are correct. My sense of intuition told me this would help you. I had no idea why, since I didn't know the nature of the dangers my fellow magicians would end up finding to throw at you on each world. But my intuition told me you'd have a better chance of survival if we spoke in this way."

Jenna's eyes widened. "*Amazing*. Your intuition is magical all right. Remembering how you and Hirth only used the literal meaning of words was a big help, especially here on Orum and while answering riddles on Mesrobia."

"I'm not trying to be critical," said Zachary, "but why didn't your intuition warn you that Hirth was about to *attack us*? That would have been good to know, too."

Wyland sighed. "It can be a frustrating talent. When I have a flash of intuition, I'm never wrong, as I mentioned. But it is all too often blank, especially where I, myself, am involved—although this isn't an absolute rule."

Zachary could see where this would be frustrating. Wyland had the *least* intuition when it came to things that affected him, personally. That hardly seemed fair. "So back to your appearance," said Zachary. "Are we seeing you now in your true form because Hirth isn't here to maintain the illusion?"

"Correct."

Zachary still found it amazing that the harmless looking creature in front of him was actually Wyland. And he couldn't help but be relieved. The appearance of the transparent men had never stopped giving him the willies. "So what are Hirth's plans?" asked Zachary.

Wyland frowned. "I don't know, but trust me, they aren't good. I've always thought he had a cruel streak and was a little unstable. But I can't believe he actually attacked a fellow member of the Grand Council. It's certain he intends to destroy the emerging portals in California."

"Then we have to go after him!" said Jenna. "Now!"

"We can't," said Wyland. "He's got us trapped." He pointed to a boulder almost fifty feet distant. Both kids could make out a crystal sitting on top of it, about the size of a human hand and shaped like a soccer ball. A glowing rainbow of color was spinning around it. "That crystal is keeping us trapped and creating a field that makes it impossible for me to use any magic. As long as it's pointing this way, we aren't going anywhere."

Zachary's face wrinkled up in disgust. Was Wyland really that lame? Just because he couldn't use magic didn't mean he couldn't use his *legs*. Zachary marched off at a brisk pace toward the crystal.

As he took his fifth step he slammed into an invisible barrier. "Ahhh" he yelled in surprise as the barrier stretched just a little and then shot him backwards like a supercharged trampoline. He landed on the ground with a painful thud.

Wyland winced. "I guess I should have told you about the walls being invisible, huh?"

Zachary lifted himself from the ground. "Yeah. That might have been *helpful*," he said with an annoyed look. "Okay. Now I get what you mean by *trapped*. So we're in some kind of invisible prison?"

"Right. A perfect square, about thirty yards on a side. Air and all other non-living matter can cross the barrier freely, but nothing that is alive can possibly get through—no matter what you try. Believe me."

Zachary was about to reply when another being who looked like a cross between a human and an Ewok flashed into existence outside the invisible barrier. He wore a robe that was similar to Wyland's, but was fiery red in color.

"Hirth, have you gone mad!" shouted Wyland at the newcomer. "What have you done?"

"Hello, *Wyland*," responded Hirth in contempt. "I'd like to say it's nice to see you, but I'd be lying."

"If you're planning to destroy the Earth's portals," said Wyland, "you'll have to answer to the entire Grand

Council. They all agreed to the test, and the course we would take if the kids passed it. They'll banish you from Orum forever, and probably much worse. You may be powerful, but not powerful enough to defeat the entire Council."

Hirth laughed. "You're a fool, Wyland. I *am* the Grand Council. But even if I weren't, we're all in total agreement. You always were the odd voice out in any discussion. And you're far too soft. We've wanted to push you off the Council for years now."

"Then why haven't you?"

"Your sense of intuition is a rare gift that has come in handy on several occasions. Not that it's helped *you* all that much," he added with a smirk. "So we kept you on the Council. But we also kept you in the dark about key pieces of information."

Jenna and Zachary could tell Wyland was reeling from Hirth's words, as though from a physical blow, but he fought off the shock and pain and stared back at Hirth defiantly. "Like what?" he demanded.

"Like the fact that we've become aware of another species. One who has been conquering worlds on a direct line that will soon lead them here. A species who can harness magic more powerfully even than we."

Wyland's eyes widened in alarm. "What?" he whispered. "And you've chosen to keep something this important from our citizens?"

Hirth nodded. "For now," he replied, his red robe glistening in the light. "Until we can study the situation further. No need to incite panic. But we believe we're in great danger from this new species. The *last* thing we need now is to deal with the Earth hatching thousands of new portals that are linked to us."

Wyland shook his head vigorously. "No, Hirth. Just the opposite is true. Humans could be our allies against this new species of magicians. If what you say is accurate, we need the humans more than ever."

"Don't you think we've thought of that? We've been studying humans for years, Wyland—not months like you thought. Earth's one working portal appeared years ago, not months. Human technology is very powerful. And while it's almost impossible to coordinate magic coming from thousands of different magicians, humans are able to coordinate their forces quite effectively." He paused. "We agreed to your test only so we could study their teamwork and problem-solving, and human behavior under stress. You hoped it would be part test and part a chance to learn more about humans. To us, they weren't being tested. They were being *studied*. To determine what kind of enemy or ally they might make."

"Even better," said Wyland. "Then you and the Council surely saw what *I* saw while observing them. That these humans would make *fantastic* allies."

"Wrong," said Hirth bluntly. "We came to the opposite conclusion. And everyone agreed."

"Impossible," said Wyland. "Not if you were watching the same kids I was." His eyes narrowed in confusion and he scratched his head. Then his already large eyes widened more than Zachary and Jenna would have thought possible. "It's because they can do magic after all, isn't it?" he said from out of nowhere.

Hirth looked stunned. "How did you know th . . . I mean, that's ridiculous," he said, trying to catch himself. But it was too late.

"How did I know that?" said Wyland. "Because I listened to Zachary and Jenna's conversation on the last world they were on. And paid attention. Zachary was able to tap into our transmission in the cave. He saw what *we* were seeing. What the crystal was showing us. For just an instant. And not with his eyes. He had to have used magic for that."

Now it was time for Zachary's eyes to widen. Jenna turned to him with her mouth open. Her brother had actually performed *magic*. Real magic. *Incredible.*

"Since I'm your prisoner," said Wyland, "you might as well tell me everything. What's the point of keeping secrets from me now?"

Hirth considered. "Since I know you can't escape, why not? We discovered that the entire Earth, for reasons we don't understand, is surrounded by a field that dampens magic. Like the field I'm using to suppress your magic right now, but slightly weaker. Even I, the most powerful magician on Orum, struggled to do the simplest magic while on Earth. I barely managed to teleport this family to the portal while I was there."

"What are you talking about?" said Jenna. "The portal just appeared in our kitchen. You didn't teleport us *anywhere*."

Hirth laughed. "Didn't I, Jenna? You know we can't open or control portals. And there is only one currently open on your world—and, trust me, it isn't in your kitchen. I put your entire family into a trance, so you would follow my instructions without knowing it. First I transported your parents to the portal and sent them through. Then I placed you in your chairs around your kitchen table, awoke you, and created the illusion of your parents disappearing in front of you."

Zachary searched his memory, but couldn't find even a hint that this had been done. If Hirth could pull off an illusion this impressive, even while suppressed, his magic was astonishing. "So you must have created the illusion of the talking bird also," said Zachary.

"Very good. I did. As the first part of the test, as you guessed. Then, when you and Jenna decided to go after your parents and stepped into what you thought was a portal, I froze you in a trance again. Then I transported you to the actual location of the portal, and sent you through."

"And my parents in the cave were an illusion also. Right?" said Jenna.

"Correct," said Hirth. "And, obviously, your parents were never on Mesrobia. When you—unexpectedly—passed their Challenge, we wanted to be sure you went where we wanted you to go. So a magician of ours caused their Chief Justice to have the illusion of speaking with one of his men, who told him he had seen your parents."

Hirth turned back toward Wyland. "Now where was I before I was interrupted?"

"You were telling me you experienced a powerful magic dampening field on Earth."

"Right. I'm the most powerful magician on Orum, and I've been refining and strengthening my magic for a lifetime. But if I had been *born* on Earth, the dampening field would have prevented me from ever taking the first step as a magician. You have to walk before you can run, and I would never have been able to walk."

"So if even *you* wouldn't have developed magic if you'd been born on Earth," said Zachary, "our lack of magic might have nothing to do with having poor minds or imaginations. It might only be because of this strange field that suppresses it."

"Unfortunately, this is true. I came to this same conclusion, and knew this was a possibility I had to test. So I forced your parents to become test subjects. They were not treated like royalty, even though this is what Wyland believed. They were put in a cold, damp cell, in complete darkness. I told them if they didn't use magic to create light for themselves, I'd let them starve to death."

"They had better still be alive," hissed Jenna, her eyes blazing with rage, now knowing that Wyland's earlier assurances meant nothing.

"They are," said Hirth. "They were finally able to produce some magic, after all. Although I had to starve them for days, and when they finally succeeded, their efforts were incredibly feeble. They were able to create a dim illumination for a few seconds at a time. It was *pathetic*," said Hirth with a sneer. "And light was the only thing they were ever able to control at all."

"Because magic is like a muscle that they've never used," said Wyland. "But with a little exercise, who knows how strong they could get?" He paused. "So what have you done with them?"

"I've erased their memory of all events since I joined them in their kitchen. And I've frozen them in another trance."

"You have to let them go!" demanded Zachary.

"I don't have to do anything!"

"Where are they?" asked Wyland.

"They're resting peacefully in a trance state only a half mile to the west of us," he said, pointing to his left.

Zachary's hands balled up into fists. If he could get his hands around Hirth's neck for just a second, *then* Hirth would see who was powerful and who wasn't.

Zachary took a deep breath and forced himself to calm down. If this journey had taught him anything, it had taught him the dangers of not keeping a clear head.

"So humans can do a little magic," he said as calmly as possible. "So what? How does that change anything? Maybe that could make us even *better* um . . . allies."

Wyland turned to him. "No, Zachary. Don't you see? Hirth has become terrified of humans. He's more afraid of your species than of the species that has been conquering worlds. Because he's guessed that your race could well turn out to be the most powerful magicians in the known universe. You've built an advanced civilization, not through the use of magic, which would have been almost effortless, but by the strength of your minds. And the strength of your collective will. You had to be able to understand things to get anything done. We didn't. Hirth knows that with time, training, and practice, your magic could be greater than our own—greater even than that of this new species of magicians threatening so many worlds."

Zachary looked at Hirth to see if he would challenge this statement, but he remained silent.

"And your people now have a deep knowledge of this thing you call science," continued Wyland. "And my intuition tells me that this gives you a huge added boost. We tap into scientific principles without knowing what they are, or how we do it. But you would know how to best take advantage of these principles. This could well make your magic more potent than any we have ever seen."

"Very good, Wyland," said Hirth. "You are exactly right. If these humans ever get off Earth and discover their potential in the realm of magic, they could be unstoppable."

Wyland nodded. "So you're intent on destroying the portals emerging on Earth, not because these children *failed*. But because they succeeded too well. They performed *too* brilliantly. Seeing these kids in action has you more afraid than ever. And you were able to convince the Council to side with you on this."

"The potential danger from these humans is beyond imagination," said Hirth. "You know I'm right. What is that infallible intuition of yours telling you?"

Wyland tilted back his head and closed his eyes for almost a minute. Finally, he frowned deeply and shook his head. "I don't know. Right now, my intuition on this subject is a blank."

"Too bad," said Hirth. "It would have been nice to have someone as talented as you side with us on this." He shrugged. "But so be it. I'm off to the Grand Council to power up the crystal that will destroy Earth's portals. And while I'm at it, we can determine what we should do with this human family. If they should live in a prison for the rest of their lives, or be executed. I'll be back in twenty or thirty minutes with a verdict, just before I isolate Earth forever."

A large black crystal emerged from one of Hirth's many pockets and began spinning by his head. "As for me," he said with a cruel gleam in his eye. "I'm going to recommend execution."

And with this said, the red-robed alien vanished into thin air.

CHAPTER TWENTY-NINE

Escape

"I'm so sorry this has happened," said Wyland. "I want you to know that most of the people of Orum are very decent. We've been the most powerful species in this section of the universe for many generations, and we've never sought to conquer others. Unlike this upstart species coming our way. I'm afraid Hirth has a cruel side. And he seems to have had an irrational reaction to your species, and has poisoned the Council against you."

"As great as it would be to discuss this right now," said Zachary, "in case you didn't hear, unless we do something, we probably only have twenty or thirty minutes left to live. So let's get out of here and figure out a way to defeat this guy. And stop him from destroying California."

"Impossible," said Wyland simply. "No one has ever escaped from this type of prison."

"*Really?*" said Zachary in amazement. "Wow, maybe we humans really *could* kick your buts," he added with just the hint of a smile. Wyland had said that while living things couldn't pass the invisible barrier, everything else could. It was time to test this out. Zachary flicked a tiny pebble at the barrier and watched it pass right through, as easily as did the air. His smile spread into a wide grin. "Well, watch carefully, because you're about to see your first escape."

Zachary turned to his sister. "I need you to gather rocks as quickly as you can and put them in a pile next to me. About the size of my hand would be good. But I need as many as you can get."

Jenna smiled as his plan became obvious to her, and she rushed off to find stones.

Wyland, on the other hand, wore a blank expression. "How will small stones help you?" he asked.

"You said all we need to do is move that crystal, right?" he said, pointing to the crystal still sitting on top of a large boulder fifty feet away.

"Right. But I've already told you. We can't reach it, and my magic won't work at all. So moving it is impossible."

Zachary shook his head. "Wow, magic really does spoil you. You really can't think of *any* other way to move that crystal?"

Wyland's brow furrowed in concentration, but he finally shook his head no, just as Jenna returned and deposited an armful of stones by her brother.

Zachary picked up one of the rocks, took careful aim, and fired it at the crystal. After a second or two of flight, Zachary's missile crashed into the large boulder on which the crystal was sitting, missing the target by several feet. He quickly picked up another and launched it at the crystal once again. There was no time to waste.

Wyland's eyes widened. Zachary guessed the alien was suddenly wondering how the people of Orum, so spoiled by being able to move things with their minds and shoot beams of energy, had never once thought of using their *arms* to launch an object at something to get it to move.

"I'm just warming up," explained Zachary as he threw another stone, missing the crystal once again. He picked up another as Jenna deposited ten more in the pile beside him. "We have a sport back home we call *baseball*—and I'm not trying to brag or anything—but I'm *really* good at it."

Zachary rifled another stone at the crystal, but it curved away at the last instant, missing by inches. If he had a few baseballs, he would have hit it by now, but the stones were odd shapes and weights and didn't fly perfectly straight.

On his eleventh try he hit the crystal dead center and it shot off the boulder into the woods, shattering as it did so.

A slow smile spread over Wyland's face and he floated five feet into the air. He caught Zachary's eye and shook his head in wonder. "That did the trick quite nicely. Thank you," he said happily. "But boy do I feel stupid," he added.

Zachary was about to say, *you should*, when he caught himself. "Nah, you just aren't used to thinking that way," he said instead, realizing as he did that it was perfectly true. "Believe me, if things were reversed—if we were on Earth and my arms were tied—I'd never think of using *magic* to move a distant object."

"Now what?" said Jenna. "Hirth won't be gone for long."

"We need a plan, and we need one fast," said Zachary. "What keeps our parents in a zombie state?" he asked Wyland. "Is it another of these crystals pointing in their direction?"

The short alien nodded.

"If we toss the crystal away, how long until they come out of the trance?" asked Zachary.

"Immediately," replied Wyland.

"Can you stop Hirth from closing our portals?" asked Jenna.

Wyland thought about this. "When he comes back, he'll have a yellow crystal with him, energized with magic from the entire Grand Council. He'll use this to close down the one active portal between our worlds and destroy the thousands about to emerge. Which will also

269

destroy your California. I can't open or move portals, as you know, but with this crystal I can block the one active portal from being used."

"So if you had this yellow crystal," said Zachary, "we could go to Earth and make sure no one else could ever follow." He paused. "If we did that, could Hirth or the Council still destroy the emerging portals? Or would they have to be on Earth to do it?"

"They'd have to at least travel to Earth to place the crystal."

"Any way to prevent this active portal from being used *without* the yellow crystal?"

Wyland frowned. "Not a chance," he said. "And that's the problem. Hirth's magic is stronger than mine. I'd be lucky to hold him off for even a short time. But I'd have to defeat him to take the yellow crystal, and that's not going to happen."

"Maybe that's true if you fight him alone," said Jenna. "But what if we work as a team? Maybe we can distract and weaken him enough for you to win."

"I think Jenna's right," said her brother. "It's the best chance we've got. The only chance. We have to get the yellow crystal from Hirth to save California. It's as simple as that. Which means we can't run. We have to stay here and throw everything we've got at him."

Jenna sighed. "Then you'd better sprint as fast as you can, Zack, and revive Mom and Dad. You're a lot faster than me, and we'll need all the help we can get."

"I agree," said Zachary. "I'll be back as soon as possible," he added, and without wasting another second he raced off toward their parents.

"Stop!" shouted Wyland at the top of his lungs.

Zachary screeched to a halt, fifteen feet away.

"My intuition is telling me we'll have a better chance of surviving if *Jenna* gets your parents," said the short alien, his blue robe shimmering in the light. "I don't know why."

Zachary considered this, but only for an instant. He wasn't about to bet against Wyland's intuition. Not now. "Jenna, go!" he shouted to his sister.

Jenna nodded, and without another word sprinted off through the woods in the direction of her parents.

CHAPTER THIRTY

Battle

Both Wyland and Zachary prepared for battle in their own way. Zachary hurriedly gathered rocks and set up piles of them behind dozens of trees and boulders, while Wyland levitated nearby, with four crystals of different colors spinning around him.

Five minutes after Zachary's preparations were complete, Hirth reappeared in a flash of light, thirty feet away, hovering above the ground.

He looked very much like a glowing, furless Ewok, yet he somehow throbbed with power, and Zachary felt terror rise up within him even greater than the terror he had felt when facing the mighty Grull. Even that all-powerful predator would have been no match for Hirth, harmless though his appearance might be.

The moment Hirth saw Wyland floating in the air, a look of astonishment came over his face. "*How did you escape?*" he demanded.

Zachary could barely breathe and felt himself trembling, but he knew he had to buy at least another five minutes before Jenna would return with their parents. With his mom and dad's memories erased, he wasn't sure how much use they would be, but the more people fighting Hirth the better chance they would have. Millions of lives were hanging in the balance.

Wyland was about to reply when Zachary jumped in ahead of him. "You were right to be afraid of us, Hirth!" he called out as loudly and confidently as he could manage. "Your crystal may have stopped Wyland's magic, but *mine* is far more potent. I was able to use it to escape your pathetic prison." He paused for effect. "*Now give me the yellow crystal and I'll let you leave here alive.*"

Hirth threw back his head and laughed. "Good try, Zachary. But I've seen you bluff before. I don't know how you escaped, but one of my talents is the ability to tell when someone has used magic recently. And you *haven't*. So forgive me for not quaking in my boots."

"Don't do this, Hirth," pleaded Wyland. "The humans can still be our allies."

"Are you kidding? Do you think the ease with which these human kids escaped my prison makes me *less* worried about their potential? Now I'm even more convinced they're too dangerous to let loose on Orum. We have to isolate their world *now*. While we still can."

"Let's talk about this," said Zachary. "I get why you're worried. How about this? How about if I volunteer to do more testing? To prove to you that we aren't a threat?"

Hirth looked around suspiciously. "Where is the girl?" he said. After a few seconds of thought he added, "She's off to free your parents, isn't she? And you're trying to stall me until she does."

Hirth shook his head in contempt. "Stall all you want, it won't do you any good. And neither will your parents. Maybe with years of practice they could challenge me. *Maybe*. But right now an Orum *infant* has stronger control of magic than they do. I can flick them away like insects. Speaking of which . . ." he added, and without warning a transparent bolt of energy shot toward Wyland at great speed, warping the air around it.

Wyland moved a crystal to block it, but some of its force got through. The residual energy from the blow sent him reeling backwards, and he crashed to the ground. His crystals dropped to the ground beside him.

"As I had expected," said Hirth calmly to his fallen fellow magician, "the Council voted to have the Lane family executed. I was going to take care of this when I returned from Earth." He shrugged. "But I guess there's no time like the present."

Hirth turned to face Zachary, but as he did so a rock slammed into his arm. He screamed in pain, his crystals momentarily dropping from the air.

Zachary quickly threw two more stones, but missed Hirth by inches both times, as the magician recovered and his crystals darted up from the ground to rejoin him.

Hirth was astonished that the human boy could propel stones with such speed and accuracy, making him unexpectedly dangerous, even without the use of magic. The magician glared at Zachary with a blistering rage and teleported to another position in the woods, forty feet from where he had been.

Zachary hadn't stopped Hirth, but he had distracted him long enough for Wyland to recover from Hirth's initial blow, and the short alien had levitated once again. A house-sized wall of smoke shot from a dark green crystal by Wyland's head and raced toward Hirth like a battering ram. This time it was Hirth who was thrown to the ground.

Zachary shook his fist triumphantly.

But this celebration was premature. Hirth recovered almost instantly, sending another invisible beam of force back at Wyland, which distorted the air even more profoundly than had the first.

This time Wyland was ready and managed to block the entire beam with a dazzling pink crystal.

Zachary hurled another rock at Hirth from behind a tree, but missed. This time, Hirth responded with a weapon of his own, firing back a bolt of lightning that scorched the sky and missed Zachary's leg by inches as he dived behind a boulder. Another pile of rocks was waiting there for Zachary and he rose and fired once more at the powerful magician.

The rock hit Hirth's forehead dead center!

At least it *should* have. But somehow the rock went right through the alien's head, not troubling him at all.

Hirth ignored Zachary and turned all of his attention to Wyland, who was firing everything he had at Hirth from multiple crystals. Smoke and light and invisible forces were exchanged between the two magicians in a hellish mask of energy and noise and destruction. Tree branches crashed, the ground shook, and the air between them became a seething, venomous hurricane whose single touch would kill a non-magician in an instant.

When the smoke cleared, Wyland was on the ground, gasping for breath, and Hirth was hovering ten feet away, looking as though he had barely been touched. "You knew you had no chance against me!" thundered Hirth. "And now you've dug your own grave!" He plucked a crystal from the air with his hand and held it toward Wyland, preparing to deliver a death blow.

Zachary raced toward Hirth, intent on tackling him. When he was seven feet away the alien diverted a small fraction of his magic to create an invisible barrier, exactly like the walls of the prison he had created earlier, and Zachary crashed into it and was thrown painfully to the ground.

Zachary would have given anything to lie on the ground until he had fully recovered, but he didn't have that luxury. If he allowed Wyland to be killed, millions of others would follow, including his entire family. He found an extra reserve of energy and will and jumped to his feet, a rock in his hand. "*Stop!*" he shouted at Hirth, his arm cocked behind his ear. "I can't miss at this range! Back off or you'll get a fastball to the head!"

Hirth just smirked and turned his back to him, focusing all of his attention on Wyland once more.

Zachary rifled the rock at Hirth's back, the invisible barrier not impeding it at all.

It was a perfect throw, but it went right through the alien magician. Zachary wasn't surprised, since Hirth hadn't been the slightest bit worried about Zachary or his rocks.

But what kind of magic was this? How could Hirth make rocks go through him? Zachary had hit the alien in the arm and had hurt him badly. But by the next rock, Hirth had made some kind of adjustment. But what? What was he missing?

The answer hit Zachary like a baseball bat to the head.

Hirth was a master of illusion.

He could make Zachary see anything he wanted him to see. After he was hit the first time, he had just made sure Zachary always saw him as being in a different place than he really was.

Energy was pouring from the crystal in Hirth's hand into Wyland, whose body was convulsing as it did so.

The short alien was sprawled on the floor of the woods and his eyes were slowly shutting, as whatever internal magic he was using to survive the onslaught was finally breaking down entirely.

Zachary's mind raced. If he didn't think of something in seconds, Wyland would die, and all would be lost.

And then he had it! He knew exactly what he had to do.

He picked up a handful of loose dirt and threw it in a wide spray to the left of Hirth. Without waiting, he picked up a second handful and threw it to his right. The particles of dirt eight feet to Hirth's right stopped in their flight, as if hitting an invisible, Ewok-sized object, while all other particles to his left and right continued on.

There you are, Hirth, thought Zachary, grabbing a rock and firing it as hard as he could, eight feet to the right of where he had been fooled into seeing the alien magician.

The stone slammed into Hirth's invisible back and sent the crystal in his hand flying. Hirth's false image eight feet away vanished, and the real Hirth screamed and fell to the ground, now clearly visible.

Wyland groaned and tried to inch behind a tree. He was still alive, but not by much.

Zachary took a few steps. The invisible barrier was down, as he had hoped.

This was his chance.

Zachary rushed forward and rifled through Hirth's glossy red robe as the alien lay stunned on the ground. In a matter of seconds he found the yellow crystal and shoved it in his own pocket.

He reached for Hirth's throat, but he was too late.

Hirth rose from the ground once again, defying gravity, and the glow came back to his body. Somehow he must have had magic that acted as body armor, softening the blow from Zack's rock and allowing him to recover far faster than he would have otherwise.

Zachary raced for cover behind a nearby boulder.

But it was too late.

An invisible force seized Zachary, lifted him into the air, and pinned him in place, ten feet away from Hirth.

"*Congratulations, Human!*" roared Hirth. "I underestimated you. I should have killed you right away rather than toying with you. But now I'm ready to take you as seriously as you deserve." His eyes blazed with an inner fire. "You've earned my undivided attention, Human," he added icily. "And I don't think you're going to like it much."

CHAPTER THIRTY-ONE

Magic

Jenna snapped her fingers in front of her zombified parents, but they continued to stare into space, as if their brains had been removed by a mad scientist. Hirth's magic trance worked better than she had expected.

Still gasping for air after her half-mile sprint, she began frantically searching for a crystal in the vicinity. After scanning the area for only forty seconds she found it. It was red with blue streaks running through it. She could have just tossed it away, but she found a large rock instead and smashed it into pieces, which was somehow more satisfying to her.

The moment the crystal shattered her parents snapped out of their trance and were fully awake, both with stunned looks on their faces.

Jenna rushed toward them and threw her arms around them, one at a time, tears streaming down her face.

"Jenna, darling, are you okay?" her mother asked anxiously, her first concern being for her daughter, but this was followed quickly by curiosity. "Where *are* we? The last thing I remember is eating dinner in our kitchen."

Her father's eyes widened. "Jenna, why does the sky look a little . . . *greenish?*"

Jenna laughed through her tears, so happy to have her parents back that she allowed herself to forget their predicament for just a moment. But she quickly returned to reality. Hirth could well have returned by now, and they didn't have a second to waste.

"I don't have time to explain," she said urgently. "But you need to follow me." She set off at a slow jog.

She looked back and her parents hadn't moved an inch, still surveying their surroundings with their mouths open. "Temporary amnesia?" said her father, trying to find some rational explanation for having no idea where he was, or how he had gotten there.

"Mom! Dad!" shouted Jenna. "I know you're confused. But we don't have time for this. If you've ever trusted me, you need to trust me now! Zachary's life is in great danger. You need to follow me NOW! It might already be too late."

Both of her parents swallowed hard. They glanced at each other. The pleading in their daughter's voice and desperate look in her eye was enough for them. They both decided they needed to take a leap of faith and do as their daughter asked, without understanding why.

Mr. Lane grabbed his wife's hand and began jogging toward Jenna. She nodded her thanks and started jogging herself, leading them back toward Zachary, and knowing her parents couldn't take a faster pace.

Jenna's mind continued to churn, far faster than her feet. She only had a few minutes to devise a strategy with two people who had no idea where they were, how they had gotten there, or what they were up against.

"I don't have time for a discussion," she called out as they jogged. "So pay close attention. And I need you to believe everything I say without question. Can you hear me?" she yelled.

Both parents yelled back that they could.

"Okay. We're not on Earth anymore. It's a long story, but your memory has been erased."

Jenna remembered that Zack had said that one of her father's friends was working on ways to control gadgets with the human brain. "This planet is very, um . . . high tech," she lied. She knew instinctively to avoid the use of the word *magic* at all costs. "They're able to broadcast some kind of signal that picks up the electricity from minds and allows you to control, um . . . light," she said, remembering that Hirth had told them this was the only thing her parents' magic had been able to affect. "You guys have already been able to do this. You just don't remember."

She paused to suck in a few deep breaths and then continued. "In just a few minutes, we'll be arriving in the middle of what will probably be a battle. We need to help. Fighting on our side will be Zack and a man who looks a little like an Ewok without any fur."

"Did you say, *Ewok?*" yelled her father in disbelief behind her, his breathing fast and irregular.

"Yes," replied Jenna. "Like from *Star Wars*."

Jenna considered telling them that millions of lives depended on this alien ally, but this would confuse them even more, so she decided against it. "We'll be fighting another man from this same species. One who can control just about everything with his mind, not just light. Our friend is wearing a blue robe, and our enemy a red one."

"Jenna, are you sure you're okay?" yelled her Mom.

"Mom, I'm fine. I know this sounds crazy. But if I were crazy, we wouldn't be on a strange world, would we? And in just a few minutes, you'll see for yourself that everything I'm telling you is true."

"I have to . . . stop for . . . a minute," said her father, barely able to get the words out. They had been jogging at a fairly slow pace, but neither of her parents were in good shape.

Jenna stopped and her parents bent over, panting, looking as if they would be sick.

Jenna was so impatient she was practically jumping out of her skin. *They needed to get there already.*

But part of her wondered if it would really matter if they did. Wyland and Zachary were going up against the most powerful magician on Orum. And what could she offer? Only her parents, totally winded and disoriented, who might have the ability—*maybe*—of controlling light a tiny bit.

If only they could control electricity. Or gravity. These were forces from which you could make weapons. True, Jenna had turned light into a weapon in the cave, but only because she had used it against a being with super sensitive vision. Now they were in bright daylight, so even if they could manage to generate an extremely bright light—a big if—this wouldn't work against Hirth.

There was only one way to use light as a weapon, and she had already found it.

She jumped as if she had been shocked.

What was she thinking? Light could be turned into the most powerful weapon of all.

A laser.

She knew all about lasers. She had just created a laser with her dad for the science fair.

Was this why Wyland's intuition had told him their chances would be better if *she* revived her parents instead of her brother? Maybe so.

She knew exactly how to turn light into a laser. The trick was that the light had to be all the same color, exactly, and it had to be something called *coherent*—which her father had explained meant organized. Instead of light waves traveling randomly, every light wave had to march in unison, exactly overlapping. Hirth didn't know anything about science, so even though his magic could easily deliver light in this precise way, he had no idea the power that this would generate.

Hirth and Wyland had been right. A knowledge of science *could* dramatically improve magic. If only her parents could do the *magic* part.

"Okay," announced Jenna. "Here's the plan. When we see the enemy I told you about, all of us need to use our minds to control the light around us. We need to get all the light waves to be, um . . . coherent."

"Like in a laser?" said her father, his breathing now more regular. "You want us to create a laser with our *minds*?"

"*Yes*," said Jenna. "You've done it before," she lied. "I can't tell you how to do it. Just take everything you know about light, and about lasers, and just imagine moving light waves so they're marching in step. And then it will happen." She paused. "Let's try it now." She pointed to a nearby tree. "All of us together imagine the most powerful laser ever. Imagine we can see the individual light waves. Then push them so they're traveling perfectly together."

Both of her parents strained as hard as they could and Jenna strained just as hard.

Nothing happened.

"We have to try harder!" insisted Jenna.

"I can't help but feel a little ridiculous," said her mother, and her father nodded his head in agreement. "You're *positive* we've done this before?" added her mom skeptically.

"*Yes!*" shouted Jenna. "Positive. If you take this absolutely seriously, I promise you it will work. Now let's try again. And really mean it this time!"

They strained for all they were worth for almost a minute, but with the same result.

Jenna frowned. "We're out of time. Let's go," she said, starting to jog once again. Even if they had no weapons, they could at least help to distract Hirth, possibly giving Wyland a chance to defeat him.

Less than two minutes later they heard a sound unlike anything they had ever heard before. As if the air itself were alive and throbbing with energy.

The three emerged from behind a tree and almost tripped over a groaning Wyland, barely alive on the ground. Fifteen feet away a second short creature was hovering in the air, and crystals were spinning around him. To their left, Zachary was suspended in the air as well, writhing in agony and gasping for breath, as if a vise was slowly crushing his chest. There was no doubt that the short alien being was somehow responsible for what was happening to Zachary.

"*Stop!*" thundered Mr. Lane, more loudly than Jenna had ever heard him yell.

"*Put down my son!*" screamed Mrs. Lane. "*Or I'll make you regret it!*"

Hirth turned to consider the new arrivals. As he did so, the invisible force holding Zachary loosened its grip just a bit, and Zachary gulped air as if he had been held underwater and had just emerged.

"Took you long enough," said Hirth calmly to the three humans. "I need another few seconds to finish off your son, and then I'll get to you. Just be patient."

"*I won't warn you again!*" said Mrs. Lane in a tone so intense that even Hirth couldn't help but shrink back for a moment.

Hirth recovered from his initial reaction and began to laugh. "Since your warnings mean absolutely nothing, I'd actually *appreciate* it if you'd stop giving them." He turned his attention back to Zachary, and once again squeezed the breath out of him. Zachary began to gasp for air like a fish out of water, seconds away from suffocating to death. "Like I said, I'll be with you very soon."

"On three," said Jenna, and her parents knew exactly what she meant. "One, two . . . three!"

Jenna and her parents strained with all of their might, willing the ability to control light to be real, pouring their hearts and minds and souls into their task in desperation. This time, they allowed no doubt to creep into their minds. Their belief that they could control light with their minds was now absolute, because it *had* to be. Zachary's life depended on it.

A beam of lava-red light as thick as a broom handle shot toward Hirth.

The beam hit the trunk of a thick tree Hirth was standing near and blasted it into oblivion, the very air around the beam catching on fire as half the tree was vaporized instantly and the other half was driven into the woods, as if it had been shot from a cannon. The sound this caused was thunderous, and nearly deafening.

Hirth was so stunned and terrified he became momentarily paralyzed, and the magic he had been using to pin Zachary ceased. Zachary dropped to the ground, finally able to breathe normally, sucking in huge lungfuls of air as fast as he could.

Wyland, his strength beginning to return, had observed the laser blast from his position on the ground near the three humans, and his mouth now hung open in utter astonishment.

Jenna and her parents were just as shocked as everyone else, unable to believe what they had created out of thin air, and still having no idea how they had done it.

Mr. Lane was the first to recover his senses and glared at a stunned Hirth with a savage intensity. "Our aim still needs a little work," he hissed. "But we won't miss the next time. Care to go another round?"

Hirth took one last look at the three humans, his eyes wide, and promptly vanished, clearly wanting no part of a magical force the likes of which had never been seen on Orum.

CHAPTER THIRTY-TWO

Earth

Jenna and her parents rushed over to Zachary, who was lying on his back where he had fallen. They each took turns hugging him as if he were a life raft in a stormy sea, tears sliding slowly down their faces. They had been seconds away from losing him forever.

"Did I ever tell you guys how much I love you?" he whispered hoarsely to his parents, his voice barely audible.

His parents both smiled and told him how much they loved him, as well.

"So is that all we have to do to get you to tell us you love us?" said Mrs. Lane, smiling through her tears, "Just create a powerful laser out of thin air to save your life from a furless Ewok? Why didn't you say so earlier?"

Zachary would have laughed but he didn't have the energy. "Saving my life was definitely a good thing," he whispered. "But you two are the best parents any kid could hope for. Even when you're grounding me."

"I couldn't agree more," said Jenna.

As much as Zachary was ecstatic that he and his family were still alive, he knew they weren't out of the woods yet. "We need to check on Wyland," he croaked, nodding in the direction of their ally. He pulled a yellow colored crystal from his pocket and handed it to Jenna.

"You did it!" shouted Jenna, brightening like a small sun. "Incredible!"

"Um . . . did what?" asked her dad.

"We'll tell you later," said Zachary. "We need to see Wyland."

Mr. Lane lifted his still-weak son from the ground and carried him the short distance to where the blue-robed alien was slowly rising from the ground. When they arrived, Zachary told his father he had regained enough strength to stand, and Mr. Lane set him down gently on his feet.

Wyland nodded to the four humans. "Now that," he whispered thinly, "was a battle. Thanks for saving my life," he said to the Lane siblings. He turned to Jenna and despite his weakened state, managed the hint of a smile. "Has anyone ever told you that you're quite the warrior?"

Jenna laughed, knowing Wyland had heard Nivek in the cave. "Yeah," she said. "I get that all the time."

"You may be the only person in history," noted Wyland, "on any world, to ever use *light* in two different ways to overcome two different, unbeatable enemies."

Mr. and Mrs. Lane glanced at each other. "I think we have more catching up to do even than we thought," said Mr. Lane.

"We have to get going," said Zachary, still not back to normal but feeling much better. "We still need to save California."

"Okay," said Mrs. Lane, raising her eyebrows. "Now I think you're just messing with us."

Zachary sighed. "I wish I were." He looked at Wyland. "Are you able to transport us all to the portal?"

Wyland was still extremely weak, and it would take him days to recover. He had been far closer to death than he wanted to admit. "I think so," he said wearily. "But only because this yellow crystal was charged up by the entire Grand Council. Otherwise, I couldn't even transport myself right now."

The short alien levitated once more and held the yellow crystal in his hand.

Suddenly, they were all in a wide open field in front of a portal, with no sensation that they had moved.

"We need to step through without delay," said Wyland. "No telling how quickly Hirth can regroup and bring reinforcements."

Once again the mouths of Mr. and Mrs. Lane were hanging open. "Uh . . . how, exactly, did we just, um . . . get here?" said Mrs. Lane.

"Magic," replied Wyland simply, and then disappeared through the portal.

"Um . . . kids," said their father. "Was he being serious? Does our alien friend really think he can do, um, you know . . . *magic*?"

Zachary raised his eyebrows. "You mean the one who can levitate and teleport? And who just disappeared through a strange portal that links planets together?"

"Well," said Mr. Lane. "When you put it like that . . ."

The four members of the Lane family stepped through the portal, and found themselves at the mouth of a cave, close enough to the entrance that they could still see quite clearly.

"Are we on Earth?" asked Mrs. Lane when they arrived.

"We're in a place called *California*," replied Wyland, trying to be helpful.

"So . . . not so much," said Mr. Lane with a grin.

"No, California is definitely part of Earth," replied Wyland.

The entire Lane family laughed. "Sorry," said Mr. Lane. "Just a little joke. Some of the people of California seem like they come from another planet sometimes. But we know they really don't."

The short alien quickly got to work making sure the portal couldn't be used any further. He held the yellow crystal in front of his huge black eyes with both hands and concentrated for several minutes. Finally, he lowered his arms and placed the crystal near the portal. He concentrated for another few minutes, made the crystal spin a number of times in the air—complaining of the near impossibility of doing magic on Earth while he did—and then reported the Earth was safe from intruders. At least for the time being.

Zachary and Jenna suddenly found themselves hugging each other in celebration, unsure of how this had happened. Both were momentarily choked up as powerful emotions of joy and relief flooded over them.

They had done it! They had found their parents and made it back to Earth. And they had stopped the most powerful magician on Orum from causing untold destruction. Both had been nearly certain they would never see their parents, or their home, ever again. But here they were. It was a glorious feeling.

Zachary thought back to the horrors they had recently encountered. He had seen a man's heart beating inside his chest. An insidious fungus had tried to make him part of it and root him to the ground. He had been in the iron grip of the cruel Grull, almost gagging from its noxious breath, while the Grull laughed about the tortures it was planning. He had been paralyzed with fear at seeing a monstrous wasp, and when he thought his fear couldn't get any greater, he had found himself blind and helpless inside a cave. And he had been seconds away from being suffocated to death by Hirth.

But despite these horrors, their travels had been *amazing*. He had had the chance to visit different *worlds*—and how many kids could say that? And he had forged friendships with a variety of marvelous beings. With Tular, armored from head to toe. With Nivek, a being whose life's experiences were so different than Zachary's that he couldn't possibly understand even the *concept* of daylight. And with Lisgar, a being with a spirit as wonderful as her initial appearance was horrifying.

And he now had incredible respect for his younger sister. He always knew deep down that they would become close when they got older, but their journeys through the portals had accelerated and deepened the process. He and Jenna would share a bond for the rest of their lives that went far beyond even that which was normally formed between a brother and sister.

As they parted after their brief hug, Jenna reflected on all they had been through as well. She had faced more horrors in a short time than she thought she would during her entire life. She had felt despair and anguish that was crippling in its intensity after Nivek had captured her brother, and she found herself in a pitch-black cave, blind, helpless, and terrified. The memory of the deep fear she had felt then and throughout their experiences would never leave her.

But that was okay, she realized. Because along with the memory of this fear came the memory of how she had overcome it. Along with all the traumatic brushes with death came the memory of how they had triumphed in each case. And *these* memories would also be with her the rest of her life. She would know that she had been unbelievably afraid but had still managed to face her fear.

And she would always remember the looks of respect she had seen on Zachary's face throughout their journey. When he had missed a riddle and instead of despairing that his only chance was his pathetic sister, he had looked to her to come up with an answer, confident that she would. And she would especially remember how he had stuck with her, knowing he would have to face the terrible and unbeatable Grull, when he could have made it through the portal.

Jenna nodded warmly at her brother. He smiled, nodded back meaningfully, and then turned to face their short alien companion. "We can't thank you enough for your help," he said. "We'll never be able to repay you."

"No need to thank me," replied Wyland, shaking his head. "You passed the test I forced you into with flying colors. You deserved a parade, not to have to fight for your lives once again. I'm just glad I could help."

"So what will you do now?" asked Zachary. "What will happen when you return to Orum?"

Wyland shook his head tiredly. "I can't return. They'll be waiting for me if I do. And waiting to storm this portal if I reopen it for even a moment. So I'm trapped here on Earth. At least for now."

Jenna turned to her parents. "He can stay with us as long as he needs to, right?"

As his father opened his mouth to speak she hurriedly added, "Before you answer, you should know that he just saved twenty or thirty million lives."

"I appreciate the kind words, Jenna," said Wyland. "But I can't take credit. Without you and Zachary, Hirth would have won for sure. You two are the most formidable team I have ever seen. It's hard to imagine any two beings working together any better."

Mr. and Mrs. Lane shook their heads as if they hadn't heard right. "Zachary and Jenna?" said Mr. Lane in amusement. "Working together rather than fighting? *Our* Zachary and Jenna?"

"Yes," replied Wyland. "Working together brilliantly."

"Wow," said Mrs. Lane with a grin. "Working together and actually hugging each other. And I thought *magic* was hard to believe."

"Yeah. Now I'm beginning to wonder if we'll *ever* catch up," added Mr. Lane.

"Don't worry, Dad," said Jenna happily. "We'll tell you everything. Now we have all the time in the world."

Zachary smiled and nodded his agreement. But in his heart he knew this wasn't true. They had survived this round, yes. But soon thousands of portals would be opening between Earth and Orum. And when they did, it would be impossible to predict what would happen next.

And there seemed to be an even more dangerous species heading their direction. One that might make their most powerful enemies on the Orum Grand Council look tame.

Zachary sighed. But that was something to worry about another day. For now, they still had a long way to travel to get home—and a lot to explain to their parents.

But one thing was certain. For good or for bad, the human race was about to enter a new age—one with endless possibilities. But also endless dangers.

"Let's get out of here," said Zachary with a sigh. He shot Jenna a warm look and a tired smile came over his face. "I think we've earned ourselves some rest."

KIDS BOOKS BY DOUGLAS E. RICHARDS

THE PROMETHEUS PROJECT: *TRAPPED* (BOOK 1)
A fantastic alien city. What wonders—and what dangers—is it hiding?

THE PROMETHEUS PROJECT: CAPTURED (BOOK 2)
When the alien city is captured and the adults are taken hostage, Ryan and Regan must thwart an unstoppable invasion.

THE PROMETHEUS PROJECT: *STRANDED* (BOOK 3)
If Ryan and Regan can survive on a hostile planet and return to Earth, they must face a ruthless adversary who controls a mysterious alien weapon.

THE DEVIL'S SWORD
A fencing tournament turns deadly! Can three young fencers thwart a plan to bring America to its knees?

ETHAN PRITCHER, BODY SWITCHER
When Ethan Pritcher switches bodies with a muscle-bound movie star, he'll need to thwart a hired killer, and his sister will need to find a way to keep the movie star, in his body, from getting kicked out of sixth grade.

ADULT BOOKS BY DOUGLAS E. RICHARDS

WIRED—A *New York Times* and *USA Today* bestseller!

AMPED—The *WIRED* sequel